CW00828461

HOLD FAST THESE FAMILY TIES

Sarah Lyndhurst is trying to adjust to her husband's recent accident and keep his joinery business ticking over. All she has been, or wanted to be, was wife to Tom and mother to their grown-up daughters, Helen, Cassie and Melanie. The role of businesswoman doesn't feel comfortable and she longs to turn back the clock. Impossible, of course. Life has changed and Sarah must change with it. But how will Tom feel about this new woman?

Books by Shirley Worrall
Published by The House of Ulverscroft:

A NEW FUTURE BECKONING
THE CALL OF THE ISLES

SHIRLEY WORRALL

HOLD FAST THESE FAMILY TIES

Complete and Unabridged

ULVERSCROFT
Leicester

First published in Great Britain in 1993

First Large Print Edition
published 2000

British Library CIP Data

Worrall, Shirley
Hold fast these family ties.—Large print ed.—
Ulverscroft large print series: romance
1. Love stories
2. Large type books
I. Title
813.5′4 [F]

ISBN 0–7089–4224–5

Published by
F. A. Thorpe (Publishing)
Anstey, Leicestershire

Set by Words & Graphics Ltd.
Anstey, Leicestershire
Printed and bound in Great Britain by
T. J. International Ltd., Padstow, Cornwall

This book is printed on acid-free paper

1

Helen Lyndhurst gave the doorbell three sharp prods, heard the shrill chimes echo through the house, then remembered that it was half-term. Her sister could be enjoying a lie-in.

Then she spotted a blue shape moving on the other side of the frosted glass panel and breathed a sigh of relief.

Melanie, wearing the blue dressing-gown that she'd had for as long as Helen could remember, opened the door. 'What's wrong?'

'Nothing's wrong, silly. I thought I'd call in on my way to the shop.' Helen paused, and then added teasingly, 'I thought I might get invited in.'

'Sorry.' Melanie moved aside. 'I just thought — '

'No. I'm just cadging a cup of tea on my way to the shop.'

There was more to her visit than that, Helen reflected, but she certainly wasn't bringing bad news. Quite the opposite in fact. She hoped to cheer Melanie up a bit.

'Is Paul at work?'

'No. He's gone to do the shopping,' Melanie told her.

'You've got him well trained,' Helen teased.

Melanie nodded, but didn't smile.

'I'll put the kettle on,' Helen suggested, 'while you go and get dressed.'

While she hunted through the cupboards for a couple of mugs, she wondered what was needed to bring a smile to Melanie's face.

Their father's accident had shaken them all but Melanie wasn't coping with it at all. She wasn't eating or sleeping, and something had to be done, if only for the sake of the child she was expecting — her first baby.

Melanie came back into the kitchen wearing a green dress with dainty embroidery on the collar and cuffs. Unfortunately, the effect was spoiled by her pale face and redrimmed, puffy eyes.

'Why don't you make an appointment to have your hair done?' Helen suggested. 'If you called at the shop afterwards, we could have lunch together.'

Melanie thought about it, but shook her head. 'Maybe next week.'

'It might cheer you up.'

'How would it cheer me up?' Melanie scoffed. 'It wouldn't get Dad out of hospital, would it?'

'Mel,' Helen said gently, 'you're getting this

2

out of proportion. Dad's coming along nicely. He's built like a bulldozer and he'll soon be up and about again. You know he will.'

'That's what they say at the hospital. But he looks awful. We called in last night and he looked — Oh, he looked awful.'

Helen wished she could argue with that, but she couldn't. She'd called at the hospital yesterday afternoon and she too had been shocked by his appearance. His skin had been a frightening shade of grey against the brilliant white of the pillow. He'd been much quieter than usual, too.

'You have to look on the bright side,' Helen said.

'Bright side?' Melanie scoffed. 'There isn't a bright side!'

'Of course there is,' Helen argued. 'It could have been a lot worse. If he'd been any closer when that load of timber shifted, it would have been more than his leg that was broken.'

'Things can always be worse,' Melanie muttered.

'Exactly! Dad's got a few cuts and bruises which will heal in no time, a couple of cracked ribs and a broken leg. It will all heal — '

'If all he has is a broken leg, Doctor Lyndhurst,' Melanie said, 'why are they operating again?'

'You know why, Mel. It isn't healing as well as they'd hoped and they're going to re-pin the bone.'

Melanie shuddered.

'After this operation, he'll soon be better,' Helen went on. 'You'll see. Look how well Mum's coping. She knows — '

'Meaning I'm not coping?' Melanie demanded.

'I didn't say that,' Helen said quietly. 'But you could put a bit more effort into life. Mum's got enough on her plate without worrying about you as well. Paul must be worried to death, too. And think of the baby, Mel. His mum should be eating well and sleeping. You should be giving him the best possible start in life.'

'Says who?' Melanie exploded. 'We're not all like you, Helen. Some of us have feelings, you know.'

'I have feelings!'

'Do you? I sometimes wonder. I haven't seen you shed a single tear since Dad's accident.'

'For goodness' sake, Melanie. Grow up!' Helen's patience had run out. 'If I thought tears would put back the clock and bring Dad home, I'd sit and weep buckets. Tears won't help anything.'

'You don't have anything to cry about!'

4

Melanie snapped back at her. 'I'm the one who's about to give up work, leaving us with a whacking great mortgage to pay on one income. Until Paul gets the video shop going — Oh yes, I know what you think about Paul. You've all been against him from the start.'

'That's not true,' Helen said, taken aback. 'Mum and Dad thought — and yes, so did I — that you weren't ready for marriage. Especially marriage to someone like Paul, but — '

'You see?' Melanie threw up her hands. 'It's always 'someone like Paul'.'

Helen took a deep breath. 'I didn't come here to argue, Mel.'

'Good, because you don't know what you're talking about. I know Paul, and you don't. He'll make a success of the video shop. None of you wanted me to marry him — '

'We thought you should wait a while,' Helen corrected her. 'You'd only known him three months when you decided to get married.'

'Three months or three years — if you'd had your way, I'd still be waiting now. But I couldn't have married a better man.' Melanie rounded on her sister. 'Just because you're older, you think you know it all. Well, let me tell you, you don't. If your bookshop closed tomorrow, it wouldn't make a scrap of difference. You don't have a family to worry about, or a mortgage to pay.'

'I know that,' Helen said, trying to calm Melanie. 'And I know it's not easy for you, but worrying won't — '

'That's just it,' Melanie cried. 'You *don't* know! You stuck your head in a few books at university, spent a couple of years working in the library, opened a bookshop, and that's it. That's your total experience of life. Books, books and more books. Tell me, has any man risked getting close enough to even kiss you?'

Helen stared back at her, hurt, bewildered and lost for words. The sound of the back door opening and closing made her jump.

'I'm back, love,' Paul called out. After dumping several bags, he came into the kitchen.

'Paul!' Melanie ran to him and buried her face in his jacket.

'Hey, what's all this about?' He frowned, looking from Melanie's bent head to Helen.

'I — I called in to cheer Mel up,' Helen said shakily, 'but I'm afraid — '

'Helen's been telling me that everything in the garden is rosy and there's nothing to worry about,' Melanie cut her off.

'And what have I been telling you?' he asked, in a teasing voice.

'How can I not worry?' Melanie cried.

6

'There's nothing to worry about,' Paul told her urgently. 'Doctor Green said you and the baby were in perfect shape, didn't he? And your dad's getting stronger every day. Everything's OK, love.'

He held her closer.

'When our baby arrives,' he promised Melanie, 'you'll look back at these silly worries of yours and laugh. You'll be showing him off to everyone. Your mum and dad will be spoiling him to death, and begging you to have evenings out so that they can have him to themselves.'

'We won't be able to afford evenings out,' Melanie murmured.

'Why on earth not?' Paul laughed. 'We'll be rushed off our feet at the shop, you mark my words. Business is improving every day.'

'Really?' Melanie asked doubtfully.

'Really.' He smiled. 'By the time the baby arrives, we'll probably be thinking about moving to a bigger house.'

'I'll be happy just so long as we can afford this one.' Melanie gave a weak smile.

'Business is good,' Paul said firmly. 'I've even been thinking about looking for a second car, for when you're at home all day.' He kissed her forehead. 'We've got everything to look forward to, darling.'

Melanie smiled at him. 'You're right. It's

just that sometimes I feel so — '

'Well don't!'

Melanie laughed and kissed him.

Helen cleared her throat to remind them that she was still there. 'I'd better get to the shop, before Joe thinks I've deserted him.' As it was her day off, Joe wouldn't think any such thing, but Helen wanted to get away.

'How's Mum?' Paul asked.

'She's at the hospital at the moment, sitting with Dad until he goes for the operation.'

'She'll cope.' Paul nodded. 'She's made of iron, that woman.'

'Mmm,' Helen agreed, but she wasn't so sure. 'Well, I must dash. 'Bye, Paul. Mel.'

Melanie's smile was a touch smug. 'Bye. Helen.'

★   ★   ★

As she cycled to the shop, (Melanie liked to laugh about her passion for cycling) Helen thought about her youngest sister. Even allowing for the attraction of opposites, she and Paul made an odd couple.

Paul had worked as a teacher for twelve months, which was when Melanie first met him, but since giving that up, he'd flitted from one madcap scheme to the next. He was currently fired with enthusiasm for his video shop, but there was no knowing how long that would last. Helen had long ago nicknamed him Gadget Man.

She could remember how her father had laughed when Paul had driven him to the house to see the latest gadget. At the press of a button from inside the car, the garage door was supposed to have opened with a flourish but, much to Paul's annoyance and his father-in-law's amusement, the gadget had failed miserably.

Helen cycled down Baker Street and stopped opposite the shop. The name, *First Editions*, was painted in dark green lettering on a pale green background. Helen was filled with love and pride every time she saw it.

She cycled round to the back entrance and tried to forget Melanie's taunts.

As soon as she stepped inside the shop, the distinctive smell of old books met her.

'It's your day off!' Her partner, Joe, greeted her in amazement.

'I know, but I had nothing better to do. Anyway, I'm taking more than my share of time off to visit Dad.'

Joe Reynolds brushed his hair back from his forehead, and smiled. 'I don't like to mention this but we're not exactly rushed off our feet.'

'True.' Helen laughed softly.

'So how is your father?'

'Fine, thanks.'

'And your mother?'

'Yes, she's fine.'

'And what about you?'

'Me? Oh, I'm fine. Thanks.'

'So everyone's fine,' Joe said drily.

Helen chuckled. 'Dad's having his operation today. We'll all feel better when that's over. Mum's got everything under control and I'm — fine.' She smiled at him. 'And how are you, Joe?'

Joe considered the question for a moment. 'I'm trying to fathom out how you can look so peaky, not to mention downright shaken, when everything is so wonderfully fine.'

His perception surprised Helen. 'I've just had words with Melanie,' she admitted. 'and it didn't do much for my morale. Still, it's not the first quarrel we've ever had and I'm sure it won't be the last. The best of it was, I only called in to cheer her up.' Not wanting to think about it, Helen changed the subject. 'Has Mrs Archer brought those books she promised me?'

Joe pointed to a large cardboard box at the back of the shop. He watched Helen go to investigate, and wondered how a person could get close to her. Or, more importantly, he wondered how *he* could get close to her.

She had a habit of shutting people out. At times, she looked vulnerable too, as if she needed someone.

'Helen — '

She looked up from the box.

'I just wanted to say that if you ever wanted to talk — well, I'm a good listener.'

That surprised her, clearly.

'Thanks, Joe. I'll bear it in mind.' She turned back to her books.

Joe couldn't see her face, it was hidden by long dark hair, but he watched her run her fingers lovingly down the spines of the books. They'd known each other for years, since their first day at university, but Joe often felt that he didn't know her at all. After graduating, they'd gone their separate ways, but still kept in touch, with phone calls and letters at Christmas.

Joe did a year's voluntary work in Birmingham, followed by two years' voluntary work in Finland. Helen took a temporary position in the town library. It should have been for three months, but she was there for two years.

'Going into business together' had started as nothing more than a joke. If they joked about it, the fact that neither of them had embarked on the promising careers they'd planned didn't seem to matter quite so much.

'It's our anniversary,' Joe remarked to break the silence, and she looked up, startled.

'Our highly successful partnership is six months old today.'

Her face lit up, as it always did when *First Editions* was mentioned. 'So it is! Six months — and we're still in business. That calls for a celebration.'

'Dinner tonight?' Joe suggested hopefully.

'I don't think the profits would stretch to that.' Helen laughed. 'I was thinking more of a cream cake with our morning coffee.'

Joe frowned. 'The invitation came from me.'

Helen gazed back at him. 'Are you inviting me out to dinner, just to celebrate six months of keeping our heads above water?'

Joe found her exasperating. He longed to tell her he was inviting her out to dinner in the slim hope of getting a little closer to her, but then —

'Isn't it worth celebrating?' he said instead.

'Yes, but — ' She paused for a moment. 'It's a nice thought, Joe, but I can't. I must see Dad.'

'We can make it later,' Joe coaxed. 'You have to eat, Helen. Besides, we need to chat about these new ideas of yours for the paperbacks.'

Joe didn't want to talk shop over dinner,

but at least he'd caught her interest.

'I'll call for you,' he suggested. 'Eight-thirty OK?'

'Yes.' She nodded. 'And thanks, Joe. It'll make a nice change.'

Without sparing it a second thought, she began taking the books out of the box.

★   ★   ★

Cassie wrote down the details of the booking she'd just taken, then rang through to the office.

'Diane, you haven't forgotten you're taking over, have you?'

'Can you give me five minutes, Cassie?'

Cassie knew that, thanks to a group of foreign businessmen who had just arrived at the hotel, the office was in chaos.

'No rush,' she assured her friend quickly. 'I'm only having lunch with Ian.'

'I suppose you're going somewhere nice.' Diane sighed. 'Think of me slaving away here with my sticky bun.'

'What happened to the diet?' Cassie chuckled.

'I'm not starting that until next week. If I had a face and a figure like yours — but there, I haven't, so I may as well indulge.'

'Actually, Ian and I have splashed out on a

bag of sandwiches to share with the ducks.'

'Last of the big spenders!' Like Cassie and Ian, Diane and her fiancé were saving to get married. 'Give me a shout when he gets here, Cassie.'

Cassie strolled over to the entrance doors. The drive was flanked by daffodils nodding their cheerful heads in the gentle breeze. She loved the daffodils and their promise of a bright year ahead.

Minutes later, a familiar rust and black Mini turned into the car park.

Ian Rhodes walked towards the hotel, deep in thought. He sprinted up the steps, and pushed open the door.

His smile was warm and reassuring, just like the one he'd given her when they'd sat next to each other on their first day at school.

'I'm here,' Diane announced, behind them. 'You can go and feed your ducks.'

'There won't be any left for the ducks.' Ian grinned. 'I'm starving.'

'You're always starving.'

They said little on the short drive and Cassie knew that, although a week had passed, their quarrel still lay between them. They'd forgiven, but neither of them had forgotten.

'I called at your place this morning, but there was no one there,' Ian said. 'I guessed your Mum was at the hospital but I thought it was Helen's day off.'

'And what would Helen do with a day off?' Cassie smiled. 'She was going to call on Melanie on her way in but apart from that, it was business as usual.'

'How is Melanie? Any better?'

Cassie shook her head.

'Mum said she left the hospital in tears last night.'

'She'll be OK. Your Mum will see to that.'

Cassie hoped so. Melanie had everything she wanted — a husband she adored, a lovely house and a baby on the way.

Cassie supposed that she would have it all, too, eventually. If Ian had his way, they'd be married tomorrow, but Cassie wanted to wait until the future was more settled. She wanted a home they could call their own, and since Ian had been made redundant, they hadn't even been able to save.

Sunlight caught the diamond and sapphire cluster she'd been wearing on her left hand for eighteen months.

Despite the sunshine, it was chilly sitting by the river. Or perhaps their unusually long silences had brought a chill to the air.

'We have to talk, Cass,' Ian said at last.

'About what?'

'You know what. And you know that I have

15

to let them know today.'

Cassie threw her sandwich to appreciative ducks. 'We've talked about it, Ian. And I honestly can't see that there's anything more to say.'

It seemed an age before Ian said, 'And I can't see how I can refuse the offer of a job.'

'But it would only be short term. You know Dad said he'd take you into the business when we were married.'

'Cass.' Ian chose his words carefully. 'It's good of your Dad, but I'm just not interested in his trade. I can think of nothing worse than spending the rest of my life worrying about the price of timber.'

Cassie stared at him, aghast. 'But everyone's assumed you'll join him.'

'I know,' Ian agreed grimly. 'But it's high time we lived our own lives instead of doing what our parents want.'

'Just because it's what they want, doesn't make it wrong,' Cassie protested. 'It would be perfect.'

'It would be hell,' Ian contradicted her fiercely. 'I don't want to be a joiner, and I refuse to spend my life indebted to your father.'

'You wouldn't be indebted to him. How can you think such a thing?'

'Cassie, I'd know I'd only got the job

16

because I was married to the boss's daughter.'

They lapsed into silence, Ian was lost in his own thoughts and Cassie simmering with anger and frustration.

'I don't see how I can turn this job down,' Ian said at last.

'But it's hundreds of miles away! London!'

'That's where the work is,' Ian said. 'The house prices are a bit steep admittedly, but with both of us working — '

'I've got a good job here!'

It was better than a 'good' job. She loved the hustle and bustle of the hotel, and she loved meeting the guests. She'd been there the day the hotel opened, she was part of it.

'There are hundreds of hotels in London, Cass. You'd soon get another job, one that you liked just as much.' Ian took a deep breath and said quietly, 'It's been a year now, and I can't sit around any longer. There just aren't any jobs for me round here, and Jon's been very good, offering this to me.'

Jon, who'd been made redundant along with Ian, had gone to London with his wife, Penny, to open their own restaurant. Cassie had thought they were out of their minds but now, just a year later, they were opening a second. They wanted someone they knew and trusted to manage the established one, leaving them free to concentrate on the new one. In short, they wanted Ian.

'We could get married right now,' Ian interrupted her thoughts. 'There's a flat above the restaurant waiting for us.'

'I don't want to live above a restaurant.' Realising she sounded petulant, Cassie took his hand. 'I'm not trying to invent difficulties, Ian, I'm just trying to be realistic. We don't have any friends down there — apart from Jon and Penny.'

'We'd soon make friends.'

'But our friends are *here*,' Cassie said. 'Our families, too. And there would be a job for you if you weren't so pig-headed.'

'Pig-headed? Just because I don't want to spend my life being patronised by your family, I'm pig-headed?'

'No. You're pig-headed and downright stupid if you imagine for one second that my family would patronise you!'

They stared at each other for a long moment.

'You'll be late for work.' Ian jumped to his feet.

Usually they strolled hand in hand, but now Cassie was struggling to keep up with Ian's furious strides.

The drive was completed in a silence.

Ian stopped the car outside the hotel, and turned to look at her.

'I'm going to ring Jon this afternoon and tell him I'll take the job.' He sounded strangely calm.

'So that's that, is it? You've made up your mind?'

'Yes.'

Cassie made four attempts at pulling his ring from her finger. When it was finally free, she hurled it at the dashboard. She couldn't see his reaction for the tears stinging her eyes, but the cool tone of his voice was enough to tear her in two.

'Are you sure this is what you want, Cass?'

Of course it wasn't, but she couldn't answer him for the huge lump that had lodged itself in her throat. She got out of the car and stumbled blindly towards the hotel.

She wasn't sure what she'd expected to happen next. It certainly wasn't for Ian to drive off without another word.

★　★　★

Sarah Lyndhurst edged the car forward with the traffic. She tried to remember if she'd eaten that day, and thought she hadn't.

She'd left for the hospital early, leaving Helen and Cassie to sort out breakfast, and driven straight from there to the yard.

What they would do without Linda, Tom's secretary, Sarah couldn't imagine. Sarah had always helped out with the accounts, but it was Linda who made sure that Tom was where he was supposed to be.

Give Tom a piece of wood and he was a genius. Give him order books or appointment books and he was hopeless. They had a lot to thank Linda for.

At the moment, she was doing a marvellous job assuring customers that Tom would soon be up and about, but even Linda couldn't stall indefinitely.

Sarah pushed all thoughts of the business to the back of her mind, and concentrated instead on the meal she'd need before going back to the hospital. If she told the girls she'd had a good lunch, she could get away with a sandwich.

And perhaps she'd sleep tonight.

She *ought* to be able to sleep. An unexpected smile flickered across her face. She ought to sleep *better* without Tom there. When she was too warm, he was cold. When she was nodding off, he was all set to chat the night away. She needed her eight hours, whereas Tom was a picture of health and vitality on five.

He'd always been full of life and vigour. The first time she saw him, he'd been pacing up and down the street, incapable of keeping still.

They'd been outside the cinema, she remembered, both pretending not to notice the other, and trying not to look at their watches in case the other suspected they'd been stood up by their dates. Several times Sarah thought he was going to suggest they watch the film together but, just when she had her polite refusal prepared, he seemed to change his mind.

So what finally possessed her to march over to him and suggest they went into the cinema together? Probably her anger at being stood up!

Tom had been so delighted that he hadn't uttered a coherent sentence all evening. Sarah, doing all the talking, had told him her life story and, after that, he was constantly finding excuses for their paths to cross.

When, slowly but surely, she fell in love with him, there had been no one more surprised than she, and no one happier than Tom.

Now, after almost thirty years of marriage, she couldn't have loved him more. He was strong, reliable, kind, thoughtful, loving . . . He was always there for her, offering one of his enormous shoulders to lean on.

Everyone saw Sarah as the driving force

behind their marriage. Friends believed that, the children believed that, even Sarah had believed it. Now she knew differently.

Without Tom by her side, Sarah was floundering hopelessly.

Perhaps she was imagining things but she felt sure the doctors were more concerned about his leg than they were letting on. She'd lost count of the 'comfortable' nights he'd spent in hospital, yet one look at Tom was enough to tell her that they'd been anything but comfortable. He looked dreadful.

Melanie wasn't looking any better, either. She'd always been Dad's girl — she'd always been a worry, too. Not for the first time, Sarah wondered how it was possible to have three such different daughters.

Helen was the quiet, dependable type who took everything in her stride. As a child, she'd loved looking after her two young sisters.

Cassie was the practical joker of the family, whose philosophy was that everything would work out right in the end, with very little effort on her part. It seemed to work, too.

Melanie was different again. There couldn't have been a more generous, loving child — so long as everything was going her way. But the tantrums she'd thrown as a youngster had been dreadful. Once she'd set her heart on something, she had to have it.

She just wished Melanie hadn't set her heart on Paul Gibson . . .

Sarah arrived home expecting to find the remains of Cassie's and Helen's breakfasts, and was pleasantly surprised to find the kitchen looking so tidy.

She made herself tea, and was about to take her first sip when the doorbell rang.

Standing on the doorstep were her neighbours, Matthew Anderson, a young widower, and his daughter, Kerry.

'We won't hinder you, Sarah,' Matthew said. 'We just wondered how Tom was.'

'Come in,' Sarah said. 'I've just made a pot of tea.' She smiled at five-year-old Kerry. 'And I expect I can find some lemonade and biscuits.'

'I'm sure you're busy.' Matthew hesitated.

'No,' Sarah told him truthfully. 'And I could do with an excuse to keep it that way.'

They went inside, and while Sarah updated Matthew on Tom's progress, Kerry helped her put biscuits on a plate.

'When's Uncle Tom coming home?' the child wanted to know.

'I don't know,' Sarah told her. 'He's having an operation today, to make his leg better, so perhaps it won't be long now.'

'I hope not. He said I could help him with the garden. And,' Kerry went on importantly, 'he said I could have my very own patch.'

Sarah knew exactly which patch he had in mind. The area beneath the dining-room window had been Helen's pride and joy, before it had been carefully split into two and then three.

Kerry, having moved away from her grandparents, looked on Tom as a sort of grandfather, and adored him. And, of course, the feeling was mutual.

When Sarah had first discovered she was expecting Helen, Tom had been hoping for a son, but his joy when presented with a daughter had known no limits. As Helen grew, and started clapping her hands with excitement every time she saw her father, his heart was lost forever. He couldn't believe his good fortune when they had a second daughter, and then a third.

Sarah hoped that their first grandchild would be a boy, but she knew Tom was hoping for a girl.

'How's your own garden coming along, Matthew?' she asked.

'Don't mention it! I'm still concentrating on the house. We haven't been in that long.'

Sarah smiled.

'It was lovely once, an absolute picture.'

Thinking about it, it seemed an odd choice of home for Matthew. His house and theirs sat like sentries on opposite sides of the lane on the edge of the village. She would have thought a place in town might have suited him better — although the garden, even in its wild state, was a perfect playground for Kerry.

From what Sarah gathered, Matthew had wanted a clean break for himself and Kerry. His wife had died four years ago, and Sarah suspected he was a long way from coming to terms with the loss.

Tom might be broken and bruised, but he was still her Tom. Matthew had lost his wife and, with her, all their dreams for the future.

'Is there anything I can do?' Matthew broke into her thoughts. 'Anything Tom needs? Anything here that needs doing?'

'There isn't,' Sarah told him, 'but thanks anyway.'

'Can we go and see him?' Kerry wanted to know.

'Of course, just as soon as he's feeling a bit better. He'll like that.' Sarah could see that Kerry didn't like that 'soon'. 'I know what he would like,' she said gently, 'a nice picture of what your patch of garden will look like. That will remind him he has to get better quickly to help you.'

Kerry was delighted to play a part in Tom's recovery. 'I'll do it tonight.'

'Are there any gardeners in the village?' Matthew asked.

'Jack Gibbs,' Sarah said immediately. 'He lives just along from the post office.'

'The blue door,' Matthew guessed accurately. 'I've noticed the garden. I'll call and see if he's interested.'

'Do that,' Sarah nodded. 'He's very good, if a bit slow. I'm afraid he spends a lot of time sitting and admiring the improvements.'

Matthew laughed. 'It will be a while before he has any improvements to sit and admire!'

★ ★ ★

Shortly after the Andersons had left, Helen pushed open the front door, shook the rain from her coat and stepped into the hall.

'I'm home, Mum!'

'And wet through, no doubt,' Sarah called back from the kitchen.

Helen went into the kitchen. 'How did you guess?'

'I could have picked you up from the shop.'

'Rain's good for the complexion,' Helen told her, 'and cycling's better for the environment.'

'And how about double pneumonia?' Sarah asked doubtfully. 'Surely you could afford a small car?'

26

'I'll think about it. But I don't go far and when I do, I can borrow yours. I like cycling, Mum. Really. Anyway, how are you?'

'Me? Do you know,' Sarah said shakily, 'you're the first person who's asked me that? I'm OK, thanks.'

'How was Dad this morning?'

'Oh, he looked — '

'As bad as he did yesterday?' Helen ventured. 'It's only to be expected, Mum. You know how he feels about hospitals. I bet this operation has got him scared out of his wits.'

'I'm sure you're right, love. He didn't look very enthusiastic about it.'

'What time are you going up there tonight?' Helen asked. 'I thought I'd keep you company for a while before Joe and I go out for something to eat.'

'You and Joe? That's nice. Going anywhere special?'

'I don't know. I left it to Joe. He said he'd call for me about half past eight.'

'He's sure to choose somewhere nice.'

'He's sure to choose somewhere that dishes up large portions.' Helen grinned. 'We're really going to celebrate six months' trading, but I'm hoping to convince Joe that we need to sell more mainstream fiction. We can still dig up the collector's items, but there's more turnover in paperbacks.'

'I'm sure there is,' Sarah nodded. 'But I thought the shop was going to be more specialised.'

'I think we can cater for all tastes.' Helen pulled a face. 'Joe doesn't but I intend to work on him.'

'Trade must be good.' Sarah smiled. 'I got through to your sisters from the yard earlier but each time I tried the shop, the line was busy.'

'The phone's busy, even if the cash register isn't.' Her smile faded. 'Did Melanie tell you we'd had words?'

Sarah was surprised. 'No. It's getting to her, isn't it? Poor Mel. By the way, how was Cassie, this morning?'

'OK. Why?'

'She sounded a bit strange when I called her this afternoon — said she'd got a cold coming.'

'That came on suddenly.' Helen frowned, reaching for the biscuit tin. 'Hey, who's eaten all the chocolate ones?'

'A tall, dark, handsome man I entertained this afternoon.' Sarah chuckled.

'Matthew?'

'So you have noticed he's tall, dark and handsome?' her mother said, straight faced.

'Oh, I've noticed.' Helen nodded. 'I'm just not quite so obvious as Cassie. And when

Melanie first saw him — Well! And her a married woman.'

Sarah laughed.

'I wonder what his wife was like,' Helen said thoughtfully.

'Beautiful,' Sarah said. 'He has a photograph of her in their sitting-room.'

'I suppose Kerry looks like her?'

'She certainly got that lovely blond hair from her mother, but no, I think Kerry's more like her father.'

'Except the eyes,' Helen said thoughtfully. 'Kerry's are the deepest shade of blue I've ever seen, and his are a warm honey colour.'

'I see,' Sarah murmured. 'And what colour eyes does Joe have?'

'I don't know! I've got better things to do with my time than gaze into people's eyes. I just happened to notice Matthew's because — '

'I know,' Sarah said gravely. 'You wondered if they were the same colour as Kerry's.'

'Yes! Honestly, I wish I'd never mentioned it.'

'I thought we could invite them for lunch on Sunday,' Sarah remarked.

'Good idea,' Helen said. 'Although Matthew won't be able to eat and keep watch on Kerry at the same time.'

'He's a little over-protective, that's all. Nice

eyes though.' Sarah teased. 'A warm honey colour, wasn't it?'

Helen gave her mother a withering glance and quickly changed the subject. 'What are you having to eat?'

'I'll have a sandwich later. I had a big lunch.'

'Perhaps we ought to get *you* to a doctor,' Helen said drily. 'You don't eat a thing in company, and yet, when you're alone, you go on these binges.'

'Yes, well — '

'You'll need your strength when Dad comes home,' Helen said. 'Remember when he sprained his ankle? He refused to rest it and then couldn't understand why it wasn't healing.'

As she spoke, Helen looked in the cupboards, hoping to find something to tempt her mother's appetite. Perhaps a tin of soup. There was some cold chicken in the fridge, too, which would make decent sandwiches.

The phone rang and she shut the cupboard door.

'That's probably Joe.'

She took the receiver from the kitchen and felt her heart do a sickly somersault as she listened to the calm voice on the other end.

'It's the hospital, Mum.' She held out the

phone for Sarah and tried to sound equally calm.

She watched the colour drain from her mother's face. Sarah didn't say a single word. She listened, and then replaced the receiver.

'Mum?' Helen prompted.

'They want me at the hospital. Right away.'

2

Sarah thought how young Doctor Patrick looked, swamped by his white coat. He looked from her to Helen and finally let his gaze return to her.

She knew the news must be bad, or she wouldn't have been summoned to the hospital like this.

'I'm afraid your husband has an embolism, Mrs Lyndhurst,' the doctor said gently.

'Is it serious?' Sarah's heart was thumping violently.

He nodded, his expression grave. 'It's very close to the brain. There's a possibility that we may have to operate.' He perched on the edge of the desk. 'I'm sorry. I wish I could tell you something positive, but at the moment, we can't say what the chances of recovery are.'

Sarah stared back at him, filled with horror and disbelief. Tom's chances of recovery! Tom was always so full of vitality, so full of life . . .

'You have to prepare yourself for a rough time ahead, Mrs Lyndhurst,' Doctor Patrick went on. 'I'm afraid the chances of your husband making a full recovery are slim.'

Sarah couldn't think straight. All she wanted was Tom.

'Can I see him?'

'Of course.' He held the door open for them. 'This has come as a dreadful shock, I know, but later, if you'd like a chat or if there's anything you're not sure about, don't hesitate to ask.'

'Thank you,' Helen murmured, as Sarah headed for her husband's room.

She wasn't sure what she expected to find there — certainly not the peaceful scene that met her. Tom, unconscious in the white bed, could have been enjoying a good night's sleep, if it weren't for the various screens and wires around him.

A young nurse got up to put two chairs by Tom's bed. Sarah supposed it was all in a day's work for her.

She turned to Helen. 'Are you OK, love?'

Helen nodded.

'Poor Tom,' Sarah murmured. 'He hates hospitals.'

'Mum — '

'Doctor Patrick's very young, isn't he?' Sarah said. 'Late thirties at the most. I expect his parents were so proud when he became a doctor but when you think about it, it's an awful job. Imagine having to tell people that — '

Sarah tasted salty tears on her lips at the exact moment that Helen's arms went around her.

'I'm all right,' Sarah said, but she clung tightly to her daughter for a few moments. 'It's the shock, that's all. I'll be all right.'

She was far from all right, but seeing the unshed tears in Helen's eyes, she knew that somehow, she had to cope with all this.

Helen took things in her stride, but the girls had never had anything like this to cope with. Cassie — always so optimistic — would be shaken to her roots. And heaven only knew what the news would do to Melanie.

With a sudden fierceness, Sarah wished it were the other way round. She wished she were lying in that bed, unaware that her life hung in the balance. Tom was so much stronger than she was . . . he would be able to look after himself and the children as well.

Everyone thought she was strong. 'Good old Sarah. She'll cope.' But good old Sarah couldn't, and the only person who would realise that was, for the first time, unable to help.

Sarah brushed away her tears.

'I'm sorry, love, I just can't stop — '

Helen clutched her hand tightly. 'It's OK, Mum. Have a good cry.'

As they held each other, their tears

34

mingling, Sarah wondered how she could ever come to terms with the knowledge that the man she loved might be lost to her forever.

★   ★   ★

Helen had added up the column of figures three times, and each time arrived at a different total. She reached for the calculator.

Joe's hand swooped down and removed it.

'Enough is enough, Helen. You're going home!'

'I'm fine.' Helen wondered how many times she'd said that during the last week. 'I should have used the calculator in the first place.'

'No,' Joe said firmly. 'You're going home, Helen. When you're not here, you're at the hospital — and all the while you're worrying about your father, your mother, Melanie and Cassie. You can't carry on like this.'

Helen knew she couldn't, but she and Joe were partners. It was only fair that she pulled her weight.

'I'd rather be here, Joe.'

'You can't do it, not today,' Joe insisted. 'You're shattered, Helen, anyone would be. You've got to go home and get some rest. Sit and put your feet up. Watch television or read a book.'

The idea brought a weary smile to Helen's face.

'It's been a week since you heard just how ill your father was — '

'And a week since I forgot about our date,' Helen interrupted him. 'I really am sorry about that, Joe. I should have let you know.'

'That's rubbish and you know it. When there's better news about your father, we'll arrange something else.' He smiled gently. 'I'm not going anywhere, you know. I'll still be here.'

Helen nodded. She could just about cope with the dashing to and from the hospital, and with the constant worry. What she couldn't bear was the kindness.

Every day brought people offering help and sympathy, and every day she saw the caring concern in Joe's eyes . . .

'You expect too much of yourself,' Joe told her. 'Go home and get some rest, or you won't be any use to anyone. When all this is over, the shop will still be here.'

Tears were threateningly close to the surface.

'I know.'

'And so will I, Helen.'

Joe had been there all the time, and she

knew he always would be. She wanted to thank him for running the shop almost single-handed, for understanding when she wanted to talk and when she wanted to be left alone.

'Thanks, Joe,' was all she could manage. 'I'll see you tomorrow.'

She shut the shop door behind her before the first tear fell.

During the cycle ride home, she managed to regain her composure, the tears drying on her cheeks.

The week's newspapers were stacked neatly on the coffee table, not one of them opened. Home had lost its cosy, lived-in look.

Taking Joe's advice, Helen made herself a cup of tea, sat down and opened that day's newspaper.

It was impossible to concentrate on world events when their own world was so threatened. She stared at the words, but all she saw was her father's smiling face.

She found herself remembering the silliest things, like the time she was seven and her pet rabbit got out. They'd searched the garden until after ten, then her mother had insisted that Helen go to bed.

'Your dad and I will keep looking,' Sarah had promised.

Helen had argued, then cried, and then

argued some more but eventually she'd gone to bed.

She was just dropping off to sleep when her father came quietly into her room with Topsy clasped safely in his large, strong hands.

'We've found him, sweetheart,' he whispered.

Then he looked at the floor and saw the enormous, muddy footprints on the pink carpet . . . He'd been so keen to reassure Helen that he'd forgotten to take his boots off.

'Your mother's going to kill me!'

Helen remembered him on her graduation day, too. Most of the people there had had children graduating along with her, but that hadn't stopped him telling everyone he met that Helen was his daughter. He had been bursting with pride — and love . . .

★　★　★

When Helen awoke, the newspaper was lying on her lap and her tea was cold. She'd been asleep for almost four hours.

A car stopped outside, and Helen went to the window, thinking it might be her mother, or one of her sisters. It turned out to be Matthew, bringing Kerry home from school.

Instead of going into their own house, their

neighbours were crossing the road towards her.

She opened the front door, and Kerry ran the last few steps.

'I've made a Get-Well card for Uncle Tom,' Kerry announced, handing over the large, poster-painted card. 'Is he better today?'

'He's the same,' Helen answered truthfully, 'but your card's lovely, Kerry. I'll take it to the hospital later and put it on the table by his bed, with your other one.'

'Isn't he even a bit better?' Kerry asked.

'These things take a long time,' Helen answered gently. 'Now, are you coming in to help me make a drink?'

She looked at Matthew. 'I was about to make a cup of tea. Can you stay and join me?'

'I'd love to, thanks,' Matthew replied. 'I'm working to an impossible deadline at the moment and I haven't stopped all day.'

Matthew wrote technical books. Helen knew he worked while Kerry was at school, and once she'd gone to bed. The rest of the time was devoted to his daughter.

'How are you all bearing up?' Matthew asked as Helen put the kettle on. 'Is there anything we can do to help?'

'There isn't, Matthew, but if anything crops up — '

'Look, my car sits idle every night,' he said.

'If it would help with hospital visits, you're more than welcome to use it. During the week all it does is ferry her ladyship here around.'

'Oh, but we couldn't!'

Helen was already overwhelmed by the neighbours' kindness. The freezer was close to overflowing with sponge cakes from Mrs Cooper, fruit cakes from Mrs Rioch, and apple pies from Miss Connolly. And Jim Stewart must have brought them every last bloom from his garden.

The cakes and pies were untouched and the flowers barely tended, but it was the thought behind the gifts that meant so much.

'You must use it,' Matthew insisted now. 'It's ridiculous to have my car parked almost outside your house.' He handed Helen a set of car keys. 'I've got a spare set at the house.'

'I don't know what to say.' She gazed at the keys in her hand.

There was no doubt about it, they had been struggling for transport. Helen had decided that she must buy a small car at the earliest opportunity, but she'd never had time.

Cassie had never bothered with a car because, in the past, wherever Cassie went, Ian usually took her. The family car was left for their mother, buzzing about between the yard and the hospital.

'It's nothing,' Matthew assured her quickly. 'If there's anything else we can do, you must say. Don't wait to be asked.'

'Thank you. Thank you very much.'

Helen was relieved to drop the keys into her skirt pocket and carry their tea and Kerry's lemonade into the sitting-room.

'Here you are, pet,' she said cheerfully, and was dismayed to find no response. Then she realised that Kerry, usually a chatterbox, was sitting on the floor, running her fingers across the carpet. She'd barely said a word.

'Did you leave your tongue at school, Kerry?' Helen asked with a smile

'I hope Tom doesn't die,' Kerry said quietly.

'Oh, Kerry.' Helen knelt on the floor beside her. 'We all hope he'll soon be better. The doctors want him to get better, and they're very clever, you know.'

'They didn't make my Mummy better,' Kerry whispered.

Helen swallowed hard.

'If your daddy dies,' Kerry said, enormous blue eyes filling with tears, 'you'll only have your mummy. And if my daddy dies, I won't have anyone at all.'

The tears spilled over, and Helen wrapped

her arms around the little girl and held her close.

'Your daddy won't die, sweetheart,' she said, her throat painfully tight.

Kerry's arms were wound tightly round her neck as the tears fell. Matthew stroked his daughter's back, silently, as if his daughter's distress was more than he could bear, and as if, like Helen, he knew there were no words of consolation.

'Your daddy's young and healthy,' Helen said, stroking Kerry's hair. 'I know Mummy died. It's very hard to bear, but it's very rare, Kerry.

'My dad isn't ill like your mummy was. He had an accident at work, and then something went wrong. He's older than your daddy, Kerry, and as we get older, it's harder for our bodies to recover from accidents.'

Kerry rubbed her tears away with her small fists. When Helen looked up, she saw that Matthew was watching her, not Kerry. Then she realised her own face was awash with tears. Not tears for her family's problems this time, but tears for a child that had learned far too early how cruel and unfair life could be.

Embarrassed, she looked away.

'The doctors are doing everything they can,' she told Kerry. 'All we can do is hope Dad — Uncle Tom — gets better.'

'I say my prayers for him every night,' Kerry confided, and Helen hugged her tight.

Kerry turned her head slightly and, tears momentarily forgotten, spoke in a matter-of-fact voice. 'There's a cat.'

Helen followed her gaze, and saw a scruffy ginger cat peering through the window at them. She lifted Kerry to her feet and took her hand.

'Come and see her. She's been visiting for over a week now. She won't come inside the house, but we often put a saucer of milk outside for her.'

'Daddy said we can have a cat soon,' Kerry said.

'I said I'd think about it,' Matthew corrected her quickly.

They poured a saucer of milk for their visitor, and Kerry insisted on sitting outside to watch. Helen and Matthew stood in the sitting-room, looking out at Kerry and the cat.

The silence was unnerving. Helen guessed they were both trying to think of something to say about Kerry's tears.

'I hate cats,' Matthew said.

The remark was so unexpected that Helen laughed.

'It's supposed to be good for children to

have pets. Gives them a sense of responsibility. And they often talk over their problems with an animal.'

The remark had brought them neatly back to Kerry's tears.

Kerry was talking to the cat, and although the animal seemed to be listening, its eyes were fixed on the saucer of milk.

'I'm sorry if Kerry's outburst upset you,' Matthew said quietly.

'Oh, it didn't! Well, only because I hate to see her so unhappy.'

'I didn't think I was going to get her to school this morning,' Matthew said. 'She's grown very — clingy.'

It was strangely touching to hear Matthew admit to worries like this. She'd always seen him as a self-confident, decisive type who had his life, and Kerry's, firmly under control.

'It must be very hard for a five-year-old to accept that she won't see her mother again,' Helen said. 'Adults can accept that these things happen. A five-year-old's life should be full of Christmases, birthday parties and days on the beach . . . '

'Kerry certainly isn't having the life we planned for her.' His smile was tinged with sadness. 'She was going to have at least three brothers or sisters, and they were all going to have the perfect childhood.'

44

That didn't seem too much to ask from life, Helen thought sadly.

'Sorry,' Matthew said, 'I didn't come here to burden you with my problems. If Kerry is a bit clingy at the moment, I expect I've only myself to blame. If we lose someone we love, we tend to cling to those we have left.'

Helen looked at him, realising for the first time just how difficult it was for him to give Kerry a normal life. She had often marvelled at Kerry's neatly-pressed dresses and shining blonde curls, but she hadn't thought of the emotional side of it.

How hard it must be for Matthew to accept that Kerry wouldn't have those brothers or sisters, that she wouldn't be able to discuss her worries with her mother, that he had to send her out to school, into the big world . . .

'It must be awful having to cope when you've lost someone so close,' she said.

'You do, though. You think you won't, but you do,' Matthew said gently. 'You get through one day at a time, and as each day passes, it gets a little less painful.'

'As a family, we've been lucky so far,' Helen admitted. 'But now, in a short space of time, everything's fallen apart. Mum's living in the past — she must have told me a dozen times about the day they met. Melanie was close to hysterics at the hospital last night.'

'What about you?' Matthew asked.

Normally Helen would have given him the same answer that she gave everyone else — that she was fine. But for some reason, she knew she couldn't fool Matthew.

'I keep remembering the little things that Dad did when I was young,' she said. 'And I can't bear the waiting. I want Dad back home, but I know that unless he can live a normal life, he'll hate it.' She paused, and thought for a moment. 'I'm terrified too,' she admitted. 'I sometimes think that only the tension is holding me together.'

Matthew nodded his understanding.

'It's the kindness that gets to me — everyone's so kind.' She looked out of the window. 'Look,' she whispered.

The cat took a cautious step forwards. It stretched its neck, licked Kerry's hand, then ran down the garden and through the hedge.

'Did you see, Daddy?' Kerry ran inside. 'The cat kissed me. Did you see?'

'I saw,' Matthew told her warily.

'Please say I can have a cat,' Kerry begged. 'I really want one, more than anything in the world.'

Helen smiled to herself. What father could resist a plea like that?

'We'll see,' Matthew said. 'There are all sorts of things to think about. For instance, what happens to it when we go on holiday?'

'Helen would feed it for us. Wouldn't you, Helen?'

'I'd love to, Kerry.' Helen couldn't help laughing, and Matthew gave her a sideways smile. 'Thank you very much! We'll go home and talk about it,' he told Kerry. 'I have the feeling I'm outnumbered here.'

'You won't forget to take my card to the hospital?' Kerry looked up and Helen ruffled her curls. 'I won't forget.'

'And take the car,' Matthew added. 'I don't need it until morning.' He hesitated, and gave a small smile. 'It's not kindness, Helen. I'm just the practical type.'

Helen stood there a long time after Matthew had gone. Something had happened between the two of them, and she wasn't sure what it was. It had started when he'd seen her tears as she'd tried to comfort Kerry. And she'd actually confessed to being terrified, and he had understood perfectly! Helen marvelled at herself. She was well aware that she held folk at arms' length. She'd always been scared to show her feelings, even to her family.

But now she'd talked to Matthew, and she felt better.

She took his car keys from her pocket. As she turned them over in her hand, she wondered how his wife must have felt, walking down the aisle knowing that Matthew was waiting for her . . .

How would a woman feel, knowing that a man like Matthew loved her?

★ ★ ★

Cassie walked up the path to the Rhodes family's house, heading for the back door.

All her life she had treated Ian's house like a second home, never bothering to knock. But everything was different now.

She retraced her steps to the front door, feeling very foolish.

She had to find out where Ian was, though.

Betty Rhodes, Ian's mother, opened the door, and Cassie was given an affectionate hug.

'Since when have you taken to knocking?' Betty asked, leading the way to the kitchen.

'I wasn't sure of the welcome I'd get,' Cassie confessed.

'You've always been welcome here, Cassie.' Betty smiled at her. 'And you always will be.'

The kitchen was a large, busy room where, ever since Cassie could remember, Ian's friends, and his brothers and sisters, had

48

gathered. Betty was always there, handing out biscuits and hot chocolate, sticking plasters and sympathy.

'Are you going to take your coat off and sit down?' Betty asked drily.

'Of course.' Cassie sat at the kitchen table, and Betty left her mountain of ironing to make coffee.

'Mum said you had a good holiday,' Cassie remarked. Ian's parents were just back from a week in Spain.

'Lovely.' Betty nodded, 'Although I'm sure you didn't come to talk about holidays.'

'No.' She took a deep breath. 'I've been trying to get in touch with Ian. He's not at the flat any longer, and — '

Betty gazed at her. 'No, love. He's in London.'

That had occurred to Cassie as a possibility, but she'd dismissed it. She couldn't believe that Ian would have packed up and gone without so much as a word.

'Does he realise just how ill Dad is?' Cassie asked.

'He'll get in touch,' Betty said, as if she could read her thoughts. 'When he's good and ready.'

'I need to talk to him now!'

'Then you should have thought of that before.' Betty sipped her coffee before she went on. 'You can't blame him for going, Cassie. The lad needs his self-respect back.

'You claimed to be in love with him, but you wouldn't marry him until you'd got the house you wanted. Good heavens, I'd have lived in a cardboard box with his father!'

'I thought it made sense to wait.' Cassie was amazed to hear Betty placing the blame squarely on her shoulders.

'If everyone waited until their dream home was furnished to perfection, there'd be precious few marriages,' Betty scoffed. 'Ian's had enough, Cassie. He needs to work, to feel he's doing something of value. In the career he wants.'

So why hadn't Ian told her he'd had enough? Cassie swallowed hard, thinking back and growing cold as she did so. He had tried to tell her — many times. She simply hadn't bothered to listen . . .

When Betty looked up again, she saw Cassie was touching one of Ian's old shirts, and tears were rolling down her cheeks.

Betty's heart softened. With her dad in hospital and no Ian to turn to, Cassie had at last found out that life wasn't always plain sailing.

She might not be the sensible, steady type that Betty would have chosen for Ian but, if she were honest, she couldn't imagine Ian finding much happiness without his precious Cassie . . .

Betty leaned over and gave her a quick hug.

'You've been so silly, Cassie.' But her voice was gentle. 'You can't give Ian his ring back one minute and expect him to come running the next.'

'I know,' Cassie sobbed, but knowing didn't make it any easier.

'Leave things be for a while.' Betty suggested. 'Think about what you really want.'

Cassie really wanted Ian. She knew that now. Ian was her whole world — her past and her future rolled into one. And now she'd lost everything.

No, it was even worse than that. Betty was right, she hadn't lost it. She'd thrown it all away.

★   ★   ★

Sarah was about to leave home for the hospital when Linda, Tom's secretary, rang the bell. Sarah knew that Helen was sitting with Tom, and Cassie would take over till Sarah was free to go.

'I've been meaning to call at the yard,' Sarah said, feeling guilty about leaving all the work to Linda. 'The days just go so fast, somehow.'

'Is there any news?' Linda asked.

Sarah shook her head. 'We just have to wait. He's still unconscious.'

'How are you coping, Sarah?'

'I'm OK,' Sarah smiled. 'The girls are marvellous, really. Melanie's finding it a strain — that's only to be expected, I suppose, with the baby to think about as well. But Cassie and Helen are coping well and everyone's trying to help.'

'Tom's very popular.' Linda smiled. 'I remember the day I started working for him. He wanted the paperwork 'tidied up', and I was so nervous. Do you know, he thanked me for everything I did and if I asked where he wanted something putting, he said, 'Wherever you think'.'

'He loathes paperwork.' Sarah chuckled.

'People always come first with Tom.'

'Yes.'

'No one could wish for a nicer boss,' Linda went on. 'He's kind, thoughtful — if anything goes wrong, he's always ready to help.'

Sarah bit her lip hard.

'Sarah, I'm so sorry,' Linda said quickly. 'I never thought — '

Sarah blinked back her tears. 'Don't be silly. You're right. Tom's so dependable. That's why it's all so hard. It's always been easier to lean on Tom, and now that he's not here — '

'Sarah — ' Linda stood up, and paced the length of the room. 'I called because I need to talk about the business. I know how you're feeling, and I've tried to wait until the time's right, but — well, the time's never right, is it?'

'Are there problems?' Sarah frowned. 'Are you over-worked? Would you like me to come in and help with the accounts?'

'It's not the accounts,' Linda answered carefully, 'and I'm far from over-worked. No, it's more serious than that, Sarah. Tom's popular, as I say, and everyone knows he does the best job, but people aren't prepared to wait indefinitely. We've lost two of our best contracts this week.'

'Two?'

'We're all dependent on the business,' Linda said urgently, 'Someone has to start making a few decisions, and soon. There's only you, Sarah.'

Sarah didn't know what to say. She couldn't even begin to think about the business.

'I'll come into the office,' she promised, 'and when Tom comes home — ' Her voice shook, but she refused to say 'if'. 'When Tom comes home, everything will sort itself out.'

'Something has to be done now,' Linda

insisted, and her tone made Sarah uneasy.

'Well — I honestly don't see what I can do.'

'Unless something is done now,' Linda said quietly, 'there won't be any business left for Tom to come home to.'

3

'Which jobs have we lost?'

'The canteen at Merriman's,' Linda replied, 'and some work at Read's, the newsagent's.'

Sarah could remember Tom talking about the job for Merriman's, the electronics factory.

'How much work have we still got?'

'That's the problem,' Linda told her urgently. 'There's hardly anything in the order book. That's why Alex and I thought you should know.'

Sarah needed time to think, and she knew she could think more clearly if she could just hold Tom's hand. The business was his domain. He and Alex Monroe, his assistant, knew between them how much the firm could tackle, without overstretching itself.

'I have to get to the hospital,' she told Linda. 'I'll come to the yard first thing tomorrow and we'll see what's to be done.' She forced a smile. 'Don't worry, Linda. We'll sort something out.'

Next morning, she still wasn't sure what,

when she, Linda and Alex were sitting in Tom's office.

'What are Richard and Mike doing at the moment, Alex?' she asked.

'They're finishing the job at Crowleys. Should be out of there at the end of the week.'

'And what's after that?'

'Just a few small jobs.' he said grimly.

'But why?' Sarah asked in amazement. 'I know we've lost Merriman's contract and Read's, and I know they were good ones, but surely Tom would have had more in hand.'

'There were two or three jobs he planned to tender for,' Alex explained. 'There was some work for the council, but the deadline for tenders was last Monday. And there was a big job for the golf club that Tom had been as good as guaranteed. Tenders for that have to be in by Friday, though.'

'The golf club? How big a job is it?'

'Very big,' Alex assured her. 'Tom saw Gerald Compton, the secretary, about it. Would have kept us going for months. The last I heard, Tom was waiting for a full spec to be sent.'

'And it hasn't come?' Sarah guessed.

'Not much point — ' Alex stopped short. 'I expect they were waiting to hear how Tom was. As he's still in hospital, they wouldn't send it, would they?'

'I suppose not,' Sarah agreed.

The telephone rang. While Linda dealt with the call, Sarah gazed out of the window at the timber piled high outside.

Did Tom feel overwhelmed by the number of people dependent on his business. There wasn't just the family to consider. Linda, in her mid-twenties, was saving hard to get married and Alex had a wife and two young children to think about. Richard and Mike also had families. The list was endless . . .

As soon as Linda had finished the call, Sarah turned to her. 'Linda, would you ring Gerald Compton, please? Ask him if he can see me this morning?'

Alex raised his eyebrows in surprise. 'I don't know what you're hoping to gain, Sarah, but Gerald Compton isn't the type to — well, I don't think he'll wait until Tom's better.'

'I don't suppose he will,' Sarah agreed, more sharply than she intended, 'but we can't sit and wait for miracles, can we?'

Linda spoke to Gerald Compton.

'He's going out in three-quarters of an hour and won't be back until tomorrow,' she told Sarah.

'Tell him I'll be there in twenty minutes.'

As Sarah drove towards the golf club, she

wondered exactly what she would say to the club secretary. She'd met him a couple of times but didn't know him well. If local gossip was to be believed, Gerald Compton's prime concern was making money and his social life was based around that ambition.

He was all smiles as he showed Sarah into his office. 'How's your husband, Mrs Lyndhurst, and can I offer you a drink?'

Sarah made a non-committal reply about Tom's health, and came straight to the point.

'There seems to have been a misunderstanding,' she said briskly. 'We've been waiting for the specification of the work you discussed with my husband.'

Making the most of his sudden loss for words, she went on, 'As tenders have to be in by Friday, I thought I'd call and collect it.'

'But Tom isn't — ' He stopped short. 'With your husband in hospital, we didn't think there was any point — he's going to be out of action for some time, surely?'

'Tom's out of action,' Sarah said firmly, 'but the business isn't.'

'Isn't it one and the same?'

'Not at all. Tom can't do everything. He doesn't price every job, hammer in every nail, drive the lorry — '

'Of course not.' Gerald Compton agreed. 'But without Tom — '

'Nothing's changed, Mr Compton.'

'Gerald.'

'Gerald.' She nodded, unable to return his smile.

'We've already had two very promising tenders,' he told her.

'And before Friday, you'll have another,' Sarah said briskly. 'We have the best reputation in the area, Mr — Gerald, and if our price is the lowest, you can rest assured that the work will be carried out to your complete satisfaction. I will personally guarantee that.'

He looked at her for several moments. Then he smiled.

'You have guts, Sarah, I'll say that for you. You're right. I shouldn't have assumed that Lyndhurst's was a one-man business. Clearly it isn't. Excuse me for a moment, won't you?'

He left the room, and came back with a printed specification.

'Remember, we've already received two very promising tenders,' he said as he handed it over. 'You'll have to be competitive.'

Sarah left him with those words still echoing in her mind. By the time she reached the yard, she was shaking.

In Gerald Compton's office, her bold claims about nothing changing in Tom's absence had sounded perfectly feasible. Now they sounded downright reckless.

Alex was in the yard, throwing tools into the back of a van, but he stopped when he saw Sarah.

'Can you spare a minute, Alex?'

'Of course.'

They went into Tom's office, and Sarah handed him the specification. He took it from her, and Sarah could see a dozen questions racing through his mind.

'You've been with Tom long enough to know how he works,' she said carefully. 'You know the cost of everything — man hours, vehicle hours, materials . . .'

'But I've never priced a job,' Alex said quickly.

Sarah had guessed as much.

'There was a time when Tom had never priced a job.'

'Yes, but — ' Alex looked at the thick wad of paper in his hands. 'This isn't exactly a small job, is it? A couple of thousand out on this one, and we'll be in it up to our necks.'

Sarah quailed at the prospect, but hid her feelings from him.

'You know the cost of everything. Your price would be the same as Tom's.'

'But, Sarah, I wouldn't know where to start.'

Sarah looked at him, and suddenly her patience snapped.

'You start where Tom would have started,' she cried. 'You think of your wife and children, and all the other people depending on this firm, and then you sit down at this desk and work out a price.'

Alex was startled by her outburst.

'I'm sorry, Alex,' Sarah said, her voice shaky. 'It's just that we need this job badly.'

'I know.' Alex gazed at the papers in his hands. 'I suppose everyone has to start somewhere.'

It was true, but a job on this scale wasn't the ideal place to start.

'I'll deliver our tender by hand on Thursday,' Sarah told him. 'You know more about this than you think, Alex. Now's the time to put it into practice.'

When he left, Sarah walked over to the window, but she saw nothing of the view outside.

To the children, she was trying to be the pillar of strength. At the hospital, she was trying to be the calm wife who understood every terrifying word they told her. Now, in Tom's office, she was trying to be the intelligent businesswoman who had all the answers.

Sarah was none of those things. She was

just a woman who wanted nothing more than to feel her husband's arms around her and hear his laughter again . . .

★ ★ ★

'It's good of you to give me a lift home, Joe.' Helen balanced several shopping bags on the back seat of Joe's car.

'The offer's always there, and you know it.' Joe drove away from the shop. 'Are you still thinking about getting a car?'

'Well, yes. I don't suppose my meagre savings will make much difference, but with Dad's business in such a state, I don't like to splash out at the moment. And with my knowledge of cars, an old wreck is out of the question.'

A car had never seemed important before, but she couldn't keep relying on Joe's generosity, or Matthew's.

Yesterday, she'd had Matthew's car all day. She'd taken Kerry to school, driven to the hospital, then to the shop, then collected Kerry from school and driven back to the hospital.

'Have you been in The Raven since the new owners took over?' Joe broke into her thoughts.

'I haven't been anywhere except home,

62

shop and hospital.'

'Now's your chance,' Joe told her. 'Rumour has it that the food's excellent. We'll sample it, shall we? It won't take long and it will save you getting something at home.'

'Well — I — '

Joe was already turning off the main road.

'You can't live on cups of tea and sandwiches, Helen.'

Helen supposed he was right. It was a relief to have a change of scenery.

They were the only customers, as it was still early. While they waited for their meal, Helen forced herself to relax.

'I saw your mum in town this morning,' Joe remarked. 'She was going into the bank.' He hesitated, and Helen guessed why.

'She looks terrible, doesn't she?'

'She's lost a lot of weight,' Joe said tactfully. 'But it's only to be expected, I suppose.'

'When she's not at the hospital, she's at the yard. I thought being involved in the business would be better for her than sitting with Dad, unable to do anything. Now I'm not so sure.'

'Keeping the business going until Tom comes home' was, Helen thought, all that was keeping her mother going.

A couple of nights ago Helen had heard her mother go downstairs. She'd looked at her clock, seen that it was almost five o'clock, and decided to investigate.

Her mother was sitting with tears pouring down her face.

'What if Tom never comes home?' she'd asked. 'What if he never comes home, Helen?'

Helen hadn't been able to give her an answer . . .

'Oh, good. Here's the food.' Joe said cheerfully.

Helen couldn't remember the last time she'd tasted anything so good. It made her think of the Sunday lunches she'd taken for granted until so recently. Their dad laughingly insisted he only married Mum for her cooking talents. Cassie and Ian were often there, clowning around. Melanie and Paul occasionally stayed for the afternoon.

'Melanie looks even worse than Mum,' Helen remarked. 'The doctor's confined her to bed. We all keep telling her that she has to rest and think of the baby, but I know perfectly well that I'd go mad stuck in bed, waiting for news about Dad that doesn't come.'

'Paul must be worried,' Joe said. 'How's the video shop faring?'

'He says it's going well. It's a shame that he isn't getting a chance to prove himself, though. He's spending time with Melanie when he knows he ought to be at the shop.'

She looked up into Joe's sympathetic eyes, and grinned suddenly.

'Sorry. I'm not very good company, am I?'

'I wasn't expecting a song and dance routine.' Joe smiled. 'When there's better news about your dad — '

'Then I'll do a song and dance routine,' Helen said lightly.

'Coffee? Or are you in a rush to get home?'

'I've got time for a coffee.' Helen was going to the hospital with Cassie, who wasn't due to finish work until later. 'This has been lovely, Joe.'

He seemed to understand that the getting away from it all for a while had been as welcome as the food.

'Then we'll have to do it more often.'

He drove her home.

'Thanks, Joe. For the lift and the food.'

'You're welcome.' Joe smiled. 'If I can't persuade you to take things easy, I can at least make you eat — cat food?'

Helen looked at the contents of her shopping bag, and laughed.

'For our visitor. The cat's calling a couple of times a day now. I almost enticed her inside yesterday, so I thought I'd try her with real food instead of milk.'

'Once you've enticed her inside,' Joe warned, 'you'll never get rid of her.'

'I know, but Kerry loves to see her. Mind you, I think our cat's calling on several houses in the neighbourhood. She used to look half-starved but she's getting fatter by the day.'

She opened the car door.

'Thanks again, Joe. I'll see you in the morning. I'll be in around nine.'

'Helen.' Joe put his hand on her arm to detain her. 'I'll be in by nine so there's no need to rush. Have a rest and come in later.'

'I'll think about it,' Helen promised.

'You can trust me,' he teased. 'I promise not to throw all those paperbacks out.'

'You'd better not.'

Helen laughed, but then the laughter died. It had been bliss to escape from the real world for an hour, but she had to return to it.

'Life's such a mess,' she whispered.

'I know.' Joe's hair had flopped across his forehead, and he brushed it away with that familiar gesture. 'If you need someone, I'm always here, Helen.'

When he leaned forward and kissed her, she was too surprised to do anything. She felt a desire to cling to him, and an equally strong desire to run.

In the end, she turned a warm shade of pink and got out of the car.

'I — I'll see you tomorrow, Joe.'

How ridiculous, she thought, as she watched him drive away. Anyone would think that she'd never been kissed. If it hadn't been so totally unexpected —

Joe was her friend, she reminded herself, and she was lucky to have such a good friend. He was incredibly perceptive to her moods. There were times when he forced her to talk, and other times when he left her alone to brood.

Without Joe, she realised with some surprise, there would be an enormous gap in her life.

$$\star \quad \star \quad \star$$

Cassie slammed the front door shut on the shower that had arrived from nowhere just in time to drench her.

'Anybody home?' she called out.

She wasn't surprised to get no answer. Not so long ago, it had been impossible to get privacy in the house, but now there was rarely anyone there.

Cassie was about to go upstairs and change out of her wet clothes when the telephone rang. Still dripping on the hall carpet, she picked up the telephone and recited their number.

'Hi, Cass.'

There were a million things she had planned to say if Ian got in touch, but she was so shocked to hear his voice that her mind went a total blank. Just when she'd given up hope of ever speaking to him again . . .

'Ian — how are you?'

'Great!'

That surprised Cassie even more.

'You?' he asked.

She certainly wasn't 'great'.

'I'm OK.'

Cassie sat on the bottom stair with the phone in her lap. 'I've seen your mum and dad a couple of times.'

'Yes, they said. I'm sorry about your dad, Cass. Mum said there was no news?'

'Not yet.' Cassie had spent almost every waking moment going over what she should say to Ian, but he sounded distant, almost like a stranger. 'We're coping, though, and perhaps no news is good news.'

'Let's hope so,' Ian agreed.

If it hadn't been for Betty, Ian's mother, Cassie would have phoned Ian long ago. She was glad now that she had waited. She had foolishly imagined that they would put their quarrel behind them and get on with living, but she was clearly wrong.

'How's your mum?' Ian asked.

A month ago, Cassie would have poured

68

out her heart to him. She would have told him that her mum was worrying herself into the next bed at the hospital.

'She's not too bad,' she said instead. 'She's trying to keep the business going. Since Dad's accident, a lot of people have cancelled work.'

'That's not surprising,' Ian replied.

Cassie was stung by the uncaring reply. Ian had told her in no uncertain terms that he wasn't interested in working for her dad, but surely he cared? Until a month ago, they'd expected to spend the rest of their lives together!

'I think the business will be all right,' Cassie said, not sure of any such thing. 'Alex Monroe has put in a tender for a job at the golf club. They're quietly confident.'

'That's good then.'

Yes, it is, Cassie felt like screaming. At least someone's doing something. She silently counted to ten.

Perhaps this call was as difficult for Ian as it was for her. After all, she'd been the one to hurl his engagement ring back at him. And he'd been the one to rush off to London without a word.

Just because this conversation wasn't going as she'd hoped, it didn't follow that Ian didn't care. He'd cared enough to pick up the telephone.

'So what about you?' she asked. 'How's London?'

'It's wonderful, Cass,' he said. 'There's so much happening. I've been busy at the restaurant, which is great, but I've also done all the tourist things — Buckingham Palace, the Houses of Parliament . . . '

'And are you enjoying work?' Cassie asked.

'The hours take some getting used to,' he admitted with a laugh. 'I rarely finish before two in the morning and often start early. I stumble around half asleep in the afternoons.'

He fell silent, and Cassie wondered if he'd guessed that she didn't want to talk about his work, or her own. She wanted to talk about them and what had gone wrong between them.

'I'm glad you called,' she said quietly.

'Perhaps I should have called before,' he said. 'I've missed you. Cass.'

'Oh, Ian. I've missed you, too. So much.'

There was a brief silence.

'Sorry, Cass, but I've got to go. We're throwing a party to celebrate tomorrow's opening of the new restaurant. Anyway, I'm glad you're all right.'

'Yes,' Cassie said, her heart pounding with hurt and anger. 'None of us are partying the nights away, but we're all right. Enjoy yourself, Ian. Goodbye!'

70

Cassie threw down the phone and blinked back her tears. What had happened to Ian?

If it was his father lying in hospital, and Betty going out of her mind with worry, Cassie would have been where she belonged, by Ian's side. She certainly wouldn't have been living it up at parties.

And what did he mean by 'we're throwing a party'? Who was 'we'? Probably Jon and Penny who owned both restaurants.

There was no law against him seeing someone else, though. Just as there was no law against her seeing someone else. But Cassie knew she could never look twice at anyone else. No one knew her as Ian did. No one made her heart quicken with a smile.

Helen had teased her about staring at Matthew as if she'd never seen a man before, but that was different. Matthew was the rare type who stands out in a crowd. All women, young or old, noticed Matthew. And most could be forgiven for dreaming a little.

Matthew wasn't Ian though.

She and Ian had shared so much over the years. Had that love been meaningless?

★ ★ ★

'I thought I'd go shopping,' Melanie announced at breakfast.

Paul, about to drink his tea, returned the cup to its saucer.

'You know what the doctor said, Mel.'

She knew, but she was tired of staying in bed. While everyone got on with their lives, she sat around bored. Paul went to the shop, Helen ran First Editions, and Cassie met interesting people at the hotel. It wasn't fair.

'And it's about time we went to see Dad,' she said.

'No,' Paul said firmly. 'There's no point, love. Your mum will let us know when there's any news.' His expression softened. 'Why not ring Helen? I'm sure she'd call in for a chat.'

'No thanks!'

Helen was the last person Melanie wanted to see. Helen would come, but along with her good advice and platitudes, she'd bring knitting patterns and wool. As far as Helen was concerned, pregnant women did nothing but knit.

'Cassie then?' Paul suggested.

'Oh yes, Cassie's great company,' Melanie said sarcastically.

'She's bound to be upset. She and Ian had been together a long time.'

'If he'd walked out on me like that, I'd consider myself well rid of him.'

'He wanted Cassie to go with him,' Paul pointed out.

'But he went anyway!'

'I'd better go, love.' Paul glanced at his watch. 'You're not to do a thing. OK? Go back to bed.'

'Why should I?' Melanie demanded.

'Because I'm asking you to.' Paul smiled, and kissed her. 'I'll try and get home early.'

Melanie felt her eyes fill with tears. She didn't want to be alone all day again.

'Will the business always come first?' she asked miserably.

Paul's eyes widened.

'The business isn't coming first. I haven't put in a full day for weeks.'

'You've brought work home.'

'I have to,' Paul said urgently. 'You know that.'

'I know that you seem to prefer working to spending time with me!'

'I'm working for you and our baby,' Paul said calmly. 'And things might be a lot better if you'd stop fretting about whether or not the doctors are doing everything they can for your dad, and start thinking about whether you're doing everything you can for our child!'

'Meaning?'

'Meaning that if you were bothered about our baby, doing as the doctor suggests might not be such a hardship!'

He hadn't closed the front door behind him before he regretted his outburst.

He hesitated on the doorstep, wondering if he should go back and apologise. But that might only make matters worse.

When he reached the shop, Susan, his assistant, was about to take the mail into his office.

Susan looked closer to fifteen than eighteen and, more often than not, could be seen frowning at her wrist as she tried to decide between two lipstick colours. She did, however, have an amazing knowledge of videos. Customers found her friendly and knowledgeable, helpful without being pushy.

'Can you hold the fort for a couple of hours this afternoon, Susan?' Paul took the mail from her.

'Of course. Melanie not well again?'

'She's a bit low.'

Paul went into his office, closed the door behind him and went through the mail.

The video business was booming, but another shop had opened closer to the main stores, and Paul had worried that their better position would take trade. His own shop was closer to the bus station, though. So far, he was all right.

When his desk was reasonably clear, he went back into the shop. Susan was taking

74

money from a customer — Neil Hutchinson.

'You can charge him extra,' Paul told Susan. Neil had been Paul's best man.

'I'll take my custom elsewhere.' Neil laughed.

'They wouldn't give you free cups of coffee,' Paul remarked.

'I thought you'd never ask. Fran's shopping, so I'm keeping out of the way for an hour or so.'

Susan brought two coffees into Paul's office and then left them alone.

'How is Fran?' Paul asked. 'And the kids? We haven't seen you for weeks.'

'They're fine, thanks. And Melanie?'

'She's OK, I suppose.'

Neil gave him a sideways glance.

'She's a bit down,' Paul told him.

'I'm not surprised.' Neil reached for his coffee. 'She must be worried about her father.'

Paul flushed with guilt, recalling the way he'd left the house that morning. 'She is. And while everyone else is dashing to and from the hospital, she has to sit at home. Mind you — '

'What?'

'We had words this morning,' Paul admitted. 'I told her to stop fretting about her dad and start worrying about the baby. You'd think that if she cared about the baby, she'd be only too happy to do as the doctor said, wouldn't you?'

Neil helped himself to a biscuit and dipped it in his coffee.

'I can't imagine that Fran would have stayed in bed. She worried me to death when she was expecting Andrew.'

'Melanie says she's bored but there's nothing she wants to do. She hates being on her own but doesn't want to see anyone.'

'Fran was moody, too,' Neil said with a chuckle. 'And Melanie's not likely to be full of the joys of spring. With her family worrying about her father, she's getting left out.'

Paul knew he was right, and he wished more than ever he hadn't been so insensitive.

'What are you hoping for?' Neil asked. 'A boy or a girl?'

'A boy would be great. But sometimes I long for a girl.' Paul smiled ruefully. 'I just wish it would hurry up and be born.'

'That time will come.' Neil laughed. 'You'll soon forget what a night's sleep is. And the expense — you wouldn't believe how quickly they grow out of clothes.'

'You're lucky, having one of each.' Paul was suddenly envious.

'Very,' Neil agreed. 'Perhaps you'll have the same. Meanwhile, I should spoil Melanie a

76

bit. Shower her with affection. Flowers, too.'

By the time Neil left, Paul was feeling far more cheerful. He'd been stupid, expecting life to carry on as normal until their baby was born. It didn't happen like that.

Neil was right — Melanie was about to present Tom and Sarah with their first grandchild, and she felt ignored.

Paul left the shop at lunch-time, called at the florist, and drove home. He was relieved, if a little surprised, to discover that Melanie must have taken his advice and gone back to bed.

'I'm home,' he called out, running up the stairs.

There was no answer and, thinking that she might be asleep, he tip-toed into their bedroom. The room was empty.

'Melanie?'

He ran downstairs and checked all the rooms. Melanie wasn't in the house.

4

Melanie's shopping bag dropped from her hand. She fell against the store window she'd been gazing into, and might have crashed to the ground if her arm hadn't been tightly grasped.

She took several deep breaths and, trembling violently, turned to thank the stranger who had come to her rescue. She felt an immense surge of relief as she found herself looking into the familiar face of Betty Rhodes, Ian's mum.

'Melanie? Are you all right, dear?'

Melanie shook her head, and then bit her lip to stem her tears.

Betty took charge at once. She picked up Melanie's bag and helped her into the shop.

'Sit down, love.'

She watched the colour slowly return to Melanie's face and then called to the shop assistant.

'Can we have a glass of water, please?'

Melanie drank the water, and decided that Cassie could have done a lot worse than Betty Rhodes as her mother-in-law.

'My car's just around the corner,' Betty

said gently. 'You sit tight while I get it. We'll have you home in no time.'

Less than five minutes later, Melanie was being ushered out of the shop, taking the good wishes of the staff with her. Their friendly enquiries as to when the baby was due, and whether she wanted a boy or a girl, had made her feel better.

It terrified her to think of what might have happened if Betty hadn't appeared. What if she'd fallen? What if she'd harmed their baby?

'Feeling any better?' Betty asked as she helped Melanie into the car.

'Much,' Melanie told her. 'And thank you, Betty.'

Betty dismissed her thanks with a wave of her hand.

'I expect you'd overdone it.'

'Yes,' Melanie agreed. 'I'm sure you're right.'

Betty weaved her way through the traffic.

'What time will Paul be home?'

'I don't know,' Melanie murmured.

That was something else she didn't want to think about, the way they'd parted that morning. His words about her looking after her health for the baby's sake sounded particularly bitter at the moment.

'If I were you,' Betty said, slowing for the lights, 'I'd have a lie down this afternoon. I'd get the doctor to call, too.'

'I might,' Melanie answered vaguely.

There had been no need to go shopping. Every day, Paul asked if there was anything she wanted. She'd left the house that morning simply to show Paul that she wouldn't take any more orders from anyone.

'Isn't that Paul's car?' Betty said, as the house came into view.

She stopped the car just as Paul ran out of the house. He was heading for his car, but he stopped when he saw them. And he looked frantic.

He didn't say anything as he helped Melanie out of the car, but she could see both fear and relief in his ashen face.

'We met in town,' Betty explained cheerfully. 'Melanie didn't feel too well. She's a bit better now, but it won't hurt to call the doctor.'

'I'm fine,' Melanie murmured, feeling like an errant child. 'And thank you again, Betty. For the lift home and for — everything.'

'Yes, thank you, Betty,' Paul said, managing a smile. 'I'll ring the doctor right away.'

'Will you come in?' Melanie asked her.

'Thanks but I'd better get back. Take care of yourself, Melanie. Bye, Paul.'

As they went inside, Melanie tried to find words to explain, and to apologise. But there were no words and she couldn't stop trembling.

Once she was sitting down, Paul stood towering above her. He waited for her to speak, and when she didn't he said, 'I'll call the doctor.'

'There's no need,' Melanie said quietly. 'It was nothing. Just a dizzy turn. And I'm better now.'

Her words did nothing to reassure him.

'He said to call him if we were worried about anything.'

'But we're not.'

'I am!'

His sharp tone silenced Melanie.

As Paul rang the Health Centre, Melanie saw the way his white knuckles gripped the receiver, and the dark shadows beneath his eyes. Did he always look so exhausted, so worried and so — old?

'Doctor Green will be here as soon as he can.' He replaced the receiver.

'I'm sorry you were so worried, Paul.'

'Couldn't you have called me? Or left a note?'

'Please don't,' Melanie whispered. 'I should have, I know, and I'm sorry. But please don't be angry.'

'I'm not angry, darling.' Paul sat beside her and took her hands in his. 'When you weren't

81

here, I didn't know what to think. But it's not just today. I worry about you, about the baby — I worry about us, as a family. You're everything to me, you and the baby. And I don't know what I can do to make things better.'

Melanie couldn't bear to be the cause of his anguish. She turned and buried her face against his shoulder.

'I know, and I'm sorry.'

Paul held her close and stroked her hair.

'I've been so wrapped up in myself,' Melanie admitted, 'I haven't realised how worried you've been. And until today, I hadn't realised that the baby is already dependent on me. I won't go off like that again.'

Paul was relieved.

'It won't be for ever, Mel. When the baby's born, you'll be your old self again.'

They clung together in silence for a moment.

'Sometimes, the baby doesn't seem real, does it?' Paul added.

Melanie gave him a watery smile.

'That's probably because we keep calling him 'it'.'

She noticed the flowers that Paul had thrown on the corner table, and looked questioningly at him.

'I'm not sure that you deserve them,' he teased.

Melanie laughed, a laugh that ended on a sigh of contentment.

'We'll be fine, Paul.'

★　★　★

'What a bargain, Helen. It's immaculate.' Cassie sat beside Helen in the smart, red Metro.

'I know, and I love it. It's lucky Joe thought of me,' Helen said as she drove towards town.

A week ago, Joe had told Helen that his elderly neighbour had decided to sell her car. It was just the bargain Joe had promised, too, in excellent condition.

It was wonderful to be independent. Helen no longer had to rely on Matthew's generosity, or bother Joe for lifts home from the shop.

'I expect he does that quite often,' Cassie murmured.

'Sorry?'

'Joe. I expect he thinks about you often. He doesn't exactly rush home from the shop to see his girlfriend, does he?'

'He doesn't have a girlfriend.'

'Exactly!' Cassie raised her eyes to the heavens. 'Honestly, I sometimes wonder where your mind is.'

'On my driving at the moment.' Helen smiled. 'And if Joe doesn't have a girlfriend, it's because we're too busy with the shop.'

'Or is it because the girl of his dreams is at the shop?'

'Girl of his dreams indeed!' Helen laughed.

Her laughter failed to conceal the warmth that flooded her face. Did Joe want more from their relationship, she wondered. Come to that, did she want more?

Sometimes she knew she did, but at other times, she was afraid that they might lose what they already had — the easy friendship, the trust, the respect.

Since he'd kissed her, their relationship had changed. Things were different. Helen couldn't hide from the fact that they were no longer just business partners.

Joe hadn't kissed her again, but Helen had caught him watching her, as if he were waiting for her to make sense of her confused thoughts.

'Do you fancy a walk through the park?' Cassie asked. 'Before we go to see Dad?'

Helen gave her a brief, curious glance. 'Good idea.'

It took five minutes to get to the park. Several people were walking their dogs but, apart from that, it was deserted.

'Do you want to talk about it?' Helen asked quietly as they walked.

'There's not much to talk about.'

'You haven't heard from Ian again?'

'No.' Her sister pushed her hands deep into the pockets of her jacket. 'Do you think he's seeing someone else?'

'Without a crystal ball, I couldn't say. But even if he were — '

'You think he is!'

'No,' Helen said carefully. 'But if he were, would it be so terrible? You might be living at different ends of the country, but what you and Ian have has taken years to build. Whether he's seeing someone else or not, Ian won't be able to forget you, Cassie. You're just as big a part of his life as he is of yours.'

'He did say he'd missed me.'

'Of course he has. I can understand him going to London,' Helen said quietly. 'With no job up here and no prospects, it must have been soul-destroying.'

'I suppose so,' Cassie agreed. 'But to go to a party — without me — '

'The ultimate crime,' Helen said drily. 'Anyway, there's nothing to stop you going out and enjoying yourself.'

The thought had occurred to Cassie several times.

'There's a party at the hotel the week after

next. I've thought of going to that.'

'Then go.'

'Oh, I don't know. It doesn't seem right when Dad's — '

'Don't be ridiculous,' Helen cut her off. 'Good grief, Dad would have a fit if he thought you'd gone into mourning! So would Mum.'

'Yes, you're right.' Cassie smiled. 'But I don't really feel like going and I don't have anyone to go with.'

Helen spluttered with laughter and Cassie grinned.

'I suppose I could find someone to take me. Hey, I could ask Matthew! That would be a feather in my cap.'

Cassie's laughter died as she spotted the expression on her sister's face.

'Grow up!' Helen said sharply. 'Matthew's got worries of his own. And he's not going to leave his little girl with a virtual stranger while he paints the town red, is he?'

'It was only a thought.'

'One I'd forget, if I were you,' Helen said stiffly. 'I doubt very much if Matthew has been to a party since his wife died four years ago.'

'Then perhaps it's time he did.' Cassie ventured.

Helen glanced at her watch.

'We ought to head back.'

Cassie lengthened her stride to catch up with her. What on earth brought that on, she wondered in amazement.

★ ★ ★

Sarah was sitting at Tom's desk, up to her eyes in paperwork, when his secretary buzzed through to say that Alex Monroe was on the phone. Tom's right-hand man had gone up to the golf club, she knew.

'Yes, Alex?'

'Sarah, I'm trying to get the plans we need for this tender.'

'And?' Sarah prompted with a frown.

There was a brief pause.

'Mr Compton isn't — '

Sarah heard two indistinct voices, and then Alex came back on the line.

'Mr Compton asked me to tell you that he'll deal with the organ grinder and not the monkey.'

'He said what!' Sarah was incredulous.

But she knew exactly what he'd said. And she knew from the anger in Alex's voice that Gerald Compton was by his side.

Sarah struggled to control her own temper.

'Well, you can tell Mr Compton that the organ grinder's on her way.'

Sarah slammed down the telephone and left the office.

Her heart was pounding with fury as she drove out to the golf club. How dare Gerald Compton treat her staff like that!

After his reluctance to consider a tender from Lyndhurst's in Tom's absence, they, along with all other interested parties, had received a letter notifying them of a late decision by the planning department. More work was now involved and those interested had been asked to re-tender.

Sarah had welcomed the news. Apart from the fact that more business was being dangled in front of them, the closing date had been extended, giving them precious time.

Sarah saw Alex and Gerald Compton as soon as she drove into the car park. They were standing by the van, Alex with his arms folded and his expression grim, and Gerald Compton looking his confident, slightly smug, self.

Sarah got out of her car and marched over to them.

'Am I to assume, Mr Compton,' she demanded, coming straight to the point, 'that you're not giving our firm the opportunity to tender?'

He was taken aback, both by the accusation

and by Sarah's obvious fury, but he soon recovered.

'Of course not. But I do prefer to deal with someone in authority.'

'Mr Monroe has all the authority you need,' Sarah assured him. 'We're professionals, Mr Compton. If he had no authority, there'd be no point in my sending him, would there?'

A smile curved the club secretary's lips, but left his eyes like ice.

'I'm a professional, too, Mrs Lyndhurst. And I'm sure you'll understand my reluctance to use a firm — what shall I say? A firm that's operating under difficult circumstances.'

Sarah wished with all her heart that she could tell Gerald Compton exactly what he could do with his job. But she couldn't afford to, and he knew it.

'The firm is operating as it always has,' she said, as calmly as she could manage. 'We have the best reputation in the area.'

'Your husband's worked hard to get that reputation,' Gerald Compton agreed.

'Naturally,' Sarah said. 'And he's employed a workforce that will make sure he keeps it. Believe me, Mr Compton, the fact that my husband is in hospital affects nothing. Mr Monroe here would be supervising this job regardless.'

Alex shifted his weight from one leg to the other. Sarah wished he would say something, but taking into account his tight-lipped expression, it was perhaps just as well that he was keeping silent.

'To your next point,' Sarah went on. 'Is your — reluctance shared by other members of the committee?'

Gerald Compton's eyes narrowed, and Sarah was elated. He might be doing the groundwork, but the final decision wouldn't be his alone.

'Perhaps I should talk to the committee?' Sarah suggested. 'I'm sure that, like yourself, they're professionals. They'll want the best job at the best price.'

'That's what we all want,' Gerald Compton agreed shortly.

'Perhaps if I explained our firm's position to them, they would be more inclined to look favourably on a tender from Lyndhurst's.'

'That won't be necessary.' He glared at her.

'Good.' Sarah smiled. 'Then perhaps you'll give Mr Monroe the information necessary for us to submit our tender. I'm sure you'll excuse me if I leave you. I have a business to run, Mr Compton.'

'Of course,' Gerald Compton muttered ungraciously.

'I'll talk to you later, Alex.' Sarah smiled. 'Call me if you have any more problems.'

'Count on it,' Alex replied. Looking six inches taller, he turned to Gerald Compton. 'I'm sure you're as busy as I am, Mr Compton, so I'll try to keep this brief.'

Sarah left them and returned to her car.

She had intended to return to the office but, instead, she took the turning that led home. Her anger, and with it her confidence, had deserted her. She felt drained.

If by any remote chance they got that job, they would have Gerald Compton breathing down their necks every minute of every day. And woe betide anyone who made a mistake.

She admitted to herself she didn't like Gerald Compton. Perhaps his high-handed rudeness wasn't aimed at her personally, but she wasn't convinced. Perhaps he didn't like the idea of dealing with a woman. But if they got the contract, he'd have to.

If they didn't get the contract, Tom's business would be virtually finished . . .

Just as Sarah stopped the car outside the house, she spotted a car in her mirror. She hoped it was a visitor for Matthew as she really couldn't cope with company.

The car stopped behind hers and, recognising the driver as Betty Rhodes, Sarah breathed a sigh of relief. Betty was an easy person to be with. She wouldn't expect a brave face or a bright smile.

'What a lovely surprise, Betty!'

'I called on the off-chance,' Betty told her, reaching inside the car for a large bouquet of flowers. 'I've driven past several times this week, but your car hasn't been here. I was going to leave these with that nice young man next door.'

She handed over the flowers.

'They're beautiful, Betty. You shouldn't have.' Sarah was touched by the unexpected gesture.

'I thought they might provide a little cheer.'

'Come and help me put them in water, Betty. We'll put the kettle on.'

While Sarah hunted for her large crystal vase, Betty made a pot of tea.

'I was about to have a good wallow in self-pity,' Sarah admitted ruefully. 'I'm glad you called.'

'No one would blame you for that.' Betty's sharp eyes took in the signs of strain in her friend. 'Has anything happened? You look — a bit jittery.'

Sarah tried to still her shaking hands as she arranged the flowers.

'Nothing important's happened. It's just the business.'

She carried the flowers into the sitting

room and Betty followed, carrying a tray.

'How's Melanie?' Betty asked.

'Like the weather,' Sarah answered with a smile. 'Sunshine and showers. But at least she seems to be doing what the doctor tells her.'

'Sarah,' Betty began carefully. 'I know you've got more than enough on your plate right now, but Melanie does need you — '

'You know what Melanie's like, Betty.' Sarah was surprised. 'She'll do exactly as she pleases. What can I do?'

'Spend more time with her,' Betty said urgently. 'We both know she's immature and a bit spoiled — but she needs to know that she's still important to you, even at a time like this.'

Sarah was stung by the criticism.

'She knows that!'

'Does she?' Betty sounded doubtful. 'I know what you're going through, Sarah — '

'No you don't,' Sarah cried. 'You can imagine how you'd feel if it was Geoff, but you don't know. You don't know what it's like to be told you could lose the only person in the world that matters to you!'

'You're right,' Betty agreed. 'I don't know what it's like. But I do know your children matter to you.'

Sarah stared at her, trying to take in her meaning. Of course the girls mattered, but they were independent now, with their own lives to lead.

'Melanie's lost her dad for the time being,' Betty pointed out gently. 'She can't lose her mum, too. You can remember how you felt when you were expecting Helen. It's exciting, but frightening. Melanie needs you, Sarah.'

'Everyone needs me. The children need me, the business needs me — ' Tears filled Sarah's eyes, blurring the cheerful display of flowers. 'And I need Tom!'

Betty gave Sarah's shoulder a gentle squeeze as the tears rolled down her cheeks.

★　★　★

Helen picked up the mail, gave the envelopes a cursory glance and left them on the hall table. It was almost seven o'clock. She and Joe had worked late, and she'd expected Cassie to be home by now, but the house was empty.

She went into the kitchen, and had her hand stretched out towards the kettle when she saw that the house wasn't as empty as she'd thought.

'Well!' Curled up on a towel that had been pulled off the radiator was the ginger cat — and four kittens. 'And I thought we were feeding you too much!'

Helen sat down, so as not to alarm their guest.

'How on earth did you get in?'

The cat, not in the least alarmed, and seemingly oblivious to her offspring, continued to lick her paw.

'You must need some food. I had no idea you were eating for five.' Helen laughed. 'And aren't they gorgeous!'

The kittens were all different. One was ginger, like its mother. Another was black, with four white socks and a white circle on its head. One was a tortoiseshell, the last a tabby. Blindly clinging to their mother, they looked so vulnerable.

Helen put some food in a bowl and milk in a saucer. She didn't expect the cat to leave her charges while she remained in the room, but she was mistaken. Their guest soon demolished food and milk before returning to the kittens.

Watching them, Helen wondered if Joe liked animals. He didn't have a pet but then, he was away from home all day. He liked children, of course. She'd seen him with young Kerry Anderson from next door.

Did Joe want children of his own? They'd been friends for years, but there were many things she didn't know about him. A month ago, she would have been able to ask him. But a month ago, his answers wouldn't have mattered so much . . .

Helen left the house and went across the road. Kerry was playing outside and she raced up to Helen.

'I've got something to show you,' Helen told her. 'Let's ask Daddy if you can come with me for a few minutes.'

Matthew came outside, and Helen experienced a familiar, almost painful, rush of pleasure at the sight of him. She couldn't explain her feelings, even to herself.

Cassie would have put it down to good old-fashioned physical attraction, but Helen prided herself on being above such things. She wasn't the type to be affected by looks alone.

'Is it OK if Kerry comes with me for a minute?' she asked him. 'There's something I want to show her.'

'It's a secret,' Kerry piped up.

'It is,' Helen agreed. 'But you can come, too, Matthew. I'm sure you'll appreciate it.'

Matthew spotted the amusement dancing in her eyes.

'I'm not sure I like the sound of this.'

Kerry held hands with both of them as they crossed the road.

'You'll have to be very quiet,' Helen warned Kerry. 'The secret is in the kitchen.'

When they reached the kitchen, Kerry forgot the need for quiet and clapped her hands with delight. The joy on her face brought a lump to Helen's throat.

'Daddy, look,' Kerry whispered. 'Aren't they the most beautiful things you ever saw?'

'Oh, absolutely,' Matthew agreed drily, a reluctant smile on his face. 'You've just made my day, Helen.'

'But aren't they sweet?' Helen chuckled.

'There's a certain appeal, but look what they'll grow into. That cat is the scruffiest animal I've ever seen!'

'She's not the prettiest cat in the world,' Helen allowed. 'What she needs is a pretty name. What do you think, Kerry?'

'Victoria,' Kerry said immediately. 'That's my middle name. Mummy chose that because it was pretty, didn't she, Daddy?'

'She did, darling.' Matthew smiled down into those large blue eyes.

'It's a lovely name,' Helen said softly. 'And so is Kerry.'

'Mummy and Daddy chose it together,' Kerry explained importantly, 'because they got me after they had a holiday in Kerry. That's right, isn't it, Daddy?'

'Yes,' Matthew replied, his smile at odds with the painful memories that clouded his eyes.

Catching Helen's sympathetic gaze on him, he said with forced lightness, 'I suppose it's lucky we didn't go to Bognor Regis.'

Kerry, unaware of anything but the cat, broke the silence. 'Can we call her Victoria then?'

'She'd like that,' Helen agreed.

'Are you going to keep all the kittens, Helen?' Kerry asked.

'We couldn't do that. We'll have to find good homes for them.'

'Daddy, we've got a good home.' Kerry's eyes were like enormous blue saucers. 'How many can we have?'

'One!' Realising what he'd said, Matthew added a resigned, 'Possibly.'

'You wouldn't want them put in a sack and dumped in the nearest river,' Helen teased.

'I'd even provide the sack.' There were tiny, humorous lines round his eyes.

'You would not!' Helen laughed. 'Anyway, it's very beneficial for children to have pets.'

'We've had this conversation before.'

So they had, a hundred years ago. Things had been bad then, but now . . . Their father was showing no sign of improvement. Melanie was currently resting in bed, struggling to keep her blood pressure down. Their mother . . .

'Helen?' Matthew's concerned voice brought her back.

'Sorry, I was miles away.'

'How many miles away?' When she didn't answer, he said softly, 'I can't bear it when you look so sad. I wish there was something I could do to help.'

Helen tried to think of something light-hearted to break the breathless silence, but her mind was a blank. All she could do was gaze into honey-coloured eyes that seemed to know her every hope and fear.

The front door opened and closed, and Cassie came into the kitchen. Matthew moved closer to Helen, to give Cassie a good view of the kittens.

What was it about Matthew? In the crowded confines of the shop, Helen and Joe were always bumping into each other, and she never gave it a second thought. Now, she was conscious of every breath Matthew took.

'We'll have to keep one, Helen.' Cassie's voice reached her. 'They're gorgeous. Are you having one, Matthew?'

'Apparently.' Matthew nodded.

Victoria watched them, quite unconcerned that she and her kittens were the centre of attention.

'I wish Dad could see them,' Cassie said wistfully.

'Me too,' Helen agreed.

'Perhaps he will soon,' Cassie said with her usual optimism. 'Let's put the kettle on, Helen. I've been rushed off my feet today — one of those days when everything that could go wrong, did. Tea or coffee, Matthew?'

'Coffee would be nice. Thanks, Cassie.'

Not for the first time, Helen thought how natural Cassie was with people. That was why she was such an asset to the hotel, she supposed. Cassie's job included the impossible task of pleasing all of the people all of the time. With her natural exuberance and sunny smile, she usually succeeded.

'Helen?'

'I'll have a coffee, too,' Helen said, getting cups from the cupboard.

'Matthew, I wonder if you'd do me a favour?' Cassie coaxed.

'That sounds ominous,' Matthew teased.

'There's a party at Hotel — '

A cup slipped out of Helen's fingers and smashed to pieces on the floor. Helen could feel her skin burning. Everyone was staring.

'Sorry,' she murmured. 'Don't touch it, Kerry, you might cut yourself.'

Helen hadn't believed for a moment that Cassie would actually ask Matthew to go to the party with her. Cassie was a natural extrovert but all the same — Helen couldn't imagine asking any man to go anywhere.

'This party,' Cassie continued, when the wreckage had been cleared away. 'It's a week on Saturday. I haven't got anyone to go with, and I thought perhaps you could take pity on a damsel in distress?'

Helen was shocked and angry. She also knew a sudden urge to throw something at Cassie.

Cassie had been born with the looks, Helen with the brains. When it came down to the really important matters, Helen decided, brains were of no use whatsoever.

'Helen will look after Kerry,' Cassie added.

'I can't promise anything,' she said sharply. 'It depends on Dad, and on Mum. Anything could have happened by then.'

'Obviously,' Cassie agreed, slightly impatiently. 'But if you can, you will, won't you?'

Helen looked at Matthew, expecting him to say there was no need to even think about it because he wasn't considering the invitation. He returned her gaze, looking a little curious.

The idea was madness. Matthew was still coming to terms with the death of his wife. Helen knew that. She'd just seen the pain in his eyes. He couldn't go out with Cassie.

They were both waiting for her answer.

'Of course I will.' Because she couldn't bear to look at Matthew, she spoke to Kerry.

'How would you like that, Kerry? We'd be all right, wouldn't we?'

'Oh, yes,' Kerry replied eagerly. 'I can show you my books, and my teddies, and everything.'

'That's settled then,' Cassie said with some satisfaction. 'So what about it, Matthew? Do we have a date?'

Helen held her breath as she waited for his answer. If he became involved with Cassie now, when Cassie was still pining for Ian, he could only get hurt.

And if Cassie became involved with Matthew when he was still missing his wife and the mother of his child, she could be even more hurt.

And if he says yes, an inner voice mocked Helen, you'll suffer more than either of them . . .

5

'I'll look forward to it, Cassie,' Matthew said. 'So long as Helen's able to stay with Kerry, of course.'

Helen was absolutely furious, but for the life of her, she couldn't provide any valid reasons why. She wasn't even sure who had made her feel that way. Cassie for issuing the invitation? Matthew for accepting? Or herself, for caring one way or the other?

She'd been convinced that Matthew would refuse. Matthew didn't relax for a second when Kerry was out of his sight. Now it seemed that all Cassie had to do was flutter her big lashes, and he'd forget he even had a daughter!

It's none of my business, Helen told herself.

Thanks to Kerry, the conversation moved on to cat baskets, and she and Matthew left soon afterwards.

Helen set about washing the coffee mugs, and prayed that Cassie wasn't about to gloat.

'You disapprove?' Cassie picked up a tea towel.

'Of what?'

'I don't know. Of my asking Matthew to the party, I suppose.'

'It's nothing to do with me.' Helen almost scrubbed the pattern off a mug.

'It's no big deal.' Cassie shrugged.

'Life generally isn't, for you.'

'What's that supposed to mean?' Cassie asked.

'Having Matthew to show off will be — what did you call it? A feather in your cap? Never mind that you're using him, or how he might feel about it.'

Cassie was momentarily speechless.

'It's only a party.' She giggled suddenly. 'We're not courting or walking out together.' She shook her head in amusement. 'Really, Helen, you read far too many historical novels.'

Helen refused to comment on that. As far as her sisters were concerned, it was a crime to read a book.

Perhaps it was absurd to believe that if she were in Cassie's shoes, about to spend an evening with Matthew, it would be — well, she wouldn't be able to shrug it off as 'only a party' or 'no big deal'.

Helen wished she could lose herself in a good book right now. Better still, she wished she was at the shop, surrounded by books, and the calm sense of normality that only

104

seemed to be found at *First Editions* these days.

A sudden picture of Joe's smiling face sprang to mind, and Helen sighed. Working with Joe wasn't as free from complications as it ought to be.

★   ★   ★

Never mind paved with gold, Cassie thought irritably, the streets of London were crammed with people who'd forgotten how to apologise when they collided with a fellow human being.

Although to be fair, she supposed her concentration wasn't at its best. Perhaps she should have telephoned.

But she hadn't come to see Ian, she reminded herself sharply. She would call at the restaurant on the off-chance but her real reason for coming to London was to enjoy a shopping spree.

She consulted her A-Z again, and saw that her next left turn should bring her onto the right road. She walked on, not stopping until she saw the name in mauve lettering. The Highlander Restaurant.

Even from this distance Cassie knew it was nothing like her mental picture of the place. It was more up-market, for one thing.

She could vaguely remember hearing Jon's and Penny's enthusiastic plans. Wanting to give the restaurant a unique touch, they'd decided to make the most of their roots and bring a touch of Scotland south of the border. They'd talked of traditional Scottish recipes, tartan napkins and Burns' Night celebrations like they'd never seen in London.

As their second restaurant was now open for business, the idea had obviously been a great success.

Before her nerve deserted her completely, Cassie strode along the pavement and stopped outside the restaurant. Through the dark windows, she could just make out customers enjoying early lunches.

She went inside and was immediately approached by a waiter, who wore a small thistle emblem on his lapel.

'A table for one?'

'I — No. I'm looking for Ian Rhodes actually. I'm a friend.'

'He won't be in until this evening,' the waiter told her.

Cassie felt relief mingled with bitter disappointment but the disappointment finally won. She hadn't come all this way for nothing, she decided, forgetting her shopping spree for the moment.

'Do you know if he's likely to be at home?'

she asked. 'His flat's above here, isn't it?'

She'd noticed windows above the restaurant but hadn't seen a way of getting there.

'He might be in.' The waiter nodded. 'Follow me. It'll be quicker to come through the kitchen.'

Out in the courtyard behind the restaurant, he showed her the flight of steps, and Cassie thanked him.

She hesitated. Even if Ian was there, he might not want to see her. Since he'd been in London, he'd only called her once.

On the other hand, it was silly not to stop and say hello . . .

Taking a deep breath, she walked up the steps and rang the bell. She could hear the radio, and Ian's cheerful, painfully familiar whistle.

Then the door opened and Cassie was face to face with him.

'Cass! What are you doing here? You should have phoned.'

His obvious pleasure at the sight of her brought sudden tears to her eyes. How she longed to throw her arms around him and tell him what a fool she'd been. If he would just say the word, she would willingly leave her home, her job and her friends for him. Without him, it all seemed meaningless.

But the warmth of his smile was at odds

with the distance he kept between them. If only he would reach out to her . . .

'I'm on a shopping binge,' she said lightly, 'and I couldn't come all this way without seeing the famous Highlander.'

'Always one for surprises,' he said with a smile. 'You look great, Cass.'

'You, too.'

They gazed at each other, searching for changes, and then Ian laughed a little selfconsciously.

'Come on in, Cass.'

Cassie followed Ian inside.

'Ian, this is lovely. The Highlander, too. It's so — '

The words died on her lips and her smile froze.

Shocked, she stared at the girl who was sitting on a kitchen stool. Tall and slim with masses of dark hair, she was deeply tanned with enormous dark eyes. The grey tights she wore showed off long, slim legs and her T-shirt was protected by a large paint-spotted shirt. She was holding a cup of coffee.

'Cassie, this is Julie,' Ian announced. 'Julie, Cassie.'

The stranger gave Cassie a long, calculating look, as if weighing up her opponent.

'Ah,' was all she said. No 'pleased to meet you' or 'Ian's told me a lot about you'. Julie turned a bright smile on Ian. 'You must have lots to talk about. I'll leave you to it.'

'Thanks, Julie.'

Did he sound reluctant?

Julie took off the shirt, threw it over a kitchen chair and left them alone. She and Cassie hadn't exchanged a single word.

'Doing a spot of decorating.' Ian finally broke the silence. 'Julie's been helping me.'

'That's nice.' Cassie was staring at that shirt.

'Yes. She's been terrific.'

'Pretty, too.'

'Her father's Italian,' Ian murmured, as if that explained everything.

Cassie didn't want to hear any more. She grabbed the shirt, resisting the almost overwhelming urge to tear it to shreds.

'I'm delighted you found a use for it,' she said, hurling the words and the shirt at him simultaneously.

Ian, too, was struggling to control his temper. He put the shirt down and folded his arms across his chest.

'She's doing me a favour. The least I could do was make sure her clothes didn't get ruined.'

'I'm sure her T-shirt would have survived the odd paint spot.'

'It's just a shirt, for heaven's sake.'

'It's a shirt I bought you!' Cassie shouted. 'And I didn't expect you to give it to one of your — '

'One of my what?' Ian demanded, his voice like ice.

'You tell me!'

'Funnily enough,' Ian snapped, 'I thought this shirt was mine to do with as I pleased. Just as the engagement ring I gave you was yours to do with as you pleased.'

'I shouldn't have come,' Cassie said, pushing past him. 'I didn't realise I'd be breaking up your cosy arrangements. I didn't realise it was off with the old and on with the new quite so quickly.'

'Cass!' Ian groaned. 'This is all wrong. Stay. We'll have lunch.'

'Lunch?' Cassie yanked the door open. 'It would choke me!'

'I can't say I'd blame it,' Ian yelled after her. 'I could cheerfully choke you myself!'

The door slammed shut and Cassie flew down the steps, along an alley and out into unfamiliar streets. She refused to cry.

Just as soon as she had her bearings, she would go and buy the most extravagant dress she could find. She would show the world — and Ian Rhodes in particular — that she couldn't care less.

Among the first people Cassie saw at the party were Geoff and Betty Rhodes. She slipped her arm through Matthew's.

'Have you met the lucky couple who narrowly escaped having me for a daughter-in-law?'

'Briefly.' Matthew nodded. 'And I'm sure they don't consider themselves lucky.'

As they made polite conversation with Geoff and Betty, Cassie saw Betty silently assessing herself and Matthew as a couple.

'I saw Ian on Thursday,' Cassie remarked. 'He seems to have settled in well.'

'Really?' Betty frowned. 'He didn't mention it.'

'It wasn't worth mentioning,' Cassie said, managing a nonchalant shrug. 'I called on him in the midst of a shopping spree, and didn't have time for more than a quick hello and goodbye.'

'Haven't you seen him tonight?' Betty was still frowning.

'Sorry?' Cassie's heart skipped a beat. 'You mean — he's here?'

'He's somewhere around.' Betty scanned the guests' faces. 'Didn't he tell you he was coming home for the weekend? He's known for a couple of weeks.'

'Well — no.'

'It's the first chance he's had to get away,' Betty explained, eyeing her curiously. 'It was only this afternoon that he decided to come along here tonight.'

'I expect we'll bump into him then,' Cassie managed to say. 'He didn't really get chance to tell me he was planning a visit.

'Matthew,' she carried on brightly, 'you must come and meet Diane. We work together.'

Fortunately, pride found Cassie a sparkling smile to wear for the evening. She still wasn't sure about the dress, though. Startling red with a black diagonal slash, it had suited the mood she'd been in when she bought it. She knew she would never be able to look at it without recalling that ill-fated trip to London.

She knew most of the people at the party. When she wasn't making lively conversation, she was dancing with Matthew, and when she wasn't doing that, she was lifting a glass to her lips as if she hadn't a care in the world.

To all intents and purposes, Cassie Lyndhurst was having a wonderful time.

'If I'd known you were such an energetic dancer, I would have let you come alone,' Matthew said with amusement as he led her away from the dance floor.

'You are enjoying yourself, aren't you?'

Cassie felt a moment's guilt.

'Of course. Although I think it's time I took you home.'

'Home? But it's still early. Besides it's Sunday tomorrow. You can have a lie-in.'

'Try telling that to Kerry,' he said drily. 'Come on, Cassie. I'm sure Ian's got the message.'

'Message?'

'That you're having fun and not sparing him a second thought.'

Cassie coloured, recalling Helen's accusation that she was simply using Matthew.

'Sorry.'

'And if you have any more to drink,' Matthew added, 'you'll have the devil of a hangover in the morning.'

He was right. Cassie felt five years old.

Her smile got her through the goodbyes, but vanished as soon as she was sitting in Matthew's car. She felt drained, and she felt terrible about ruining Matthew's evening. He was good company. She shouldn't have needed to pretend that she was enjoying herself.

But in her wildest dreams, she hadn't imagined that Ian would be there.

Matthew stopped the car outside their houses and then took Cassie's hand as he walked her to her door.

'I'm sorry I ruined your evening,' Cassie blurted out. 'It was just with Ian being there — I'm afraid I wasn't really in the mood.'

'You didn't ruin my evening,' Matthew assured her. 'You're a delightful companion. But that isn't the way to do it, Cassie. You can't keep smiling when your eyes are full of tears.'

'I'm sorry,' she said again.

'Don't be. And if you want company again, you know where I am.'

The kind words brought tears of humiliation to her eyes.

'I've made a right fool of myself, haven't I?'

'Of course not.' Matthew smiled. 'But why not channel your energy into sorting things out with Ian? Instead of pretending that he doesn't exist, couldn't you have tried talking to him? Can't you tell him how you feel?'

'No. I'm not even sure how I feel any more. But there's nothing to sort out. It's all over.' She managed a smile. 'I don't suppose Ian's the type you can throw engagement rings back at.'

'Few men are.' Matthew grimaced.

'No.'

'If it is all over, Cassie, give yourself time to get over it.'

Cassie couldn't imagine ever 'getting over it'. Ian had been in her life for too long.

'Are you coming in?' she asked.

'No thanks. I'd better go and rescue your sister.'

'Thanks, Matthew . . . for everything.'

'You're welcome. And don't go crying into your pillow, OK? You'll look terrible in the morning, and that won't do my ego any good at all.'

Cassie laughed and on a sudden impulse, threw her arms around his neck. 'You really are very nice, Matthew.'

'That's me, Mister Nice Guy.' He kissed her forehead. 'Goodnight, Cassie.'

$$\star \quad \star \quad \star$$

Helen was standing in the sitting-room when Matthew got in. Try as she might she couldn't stop shaking.

She'd just gone upstairs to check on Kerry when she heard the car pull up. She'd gone to the window, thinking it was too early for Matthew and Cassie, and had been surprised to see them cross the road, hand in hand.

She'd seen it all as they'd stood bathed in the light from the porch. She'd seen Cassie throw her arms around Matthew. She'd seen Matthew bend his head to kiss her . . .

As she heard him come through the front

door, she sat down, but immediately sprang to her feet again.

She heard him drop his car keys on to the hall table, and then he was in the room.

'Everything OK?'

'Fine. Kerry behaved impeccably. Although she was a little late going to bed, I'm afraid.'

'That figures,' Matthew said with a smile.

'How about you? Did you have a good time?'

'It had its moments,' he replied drily. 'Ian was there.'

'Ian?'

Matthew nodded.

'According to Betty, he'd been planning this weekend for a couple of weeks.'

'But I thought — did Cassie know?'

'No.'

'Oh Lord! They didn't — '

'No scenes,' he assured her with a smile. 'In fact, they spent the entire evening studiously avoiding each other.'

'And is Cassie all right?'

'I think so,' Matthew replied. 'Anyway, let me put the kettle on.'

'Not for me,' Helen said quickly.

That seemed to annoy him.

'Helen, I'm a good hour earlier than you expected. You don't have to rush away.'

'No.' The refusal had sounded rude, she

116

realised. And if she rushed home, she would only have to listen to Cassie's version of the evening. ' 'Thank you. Coffee would be nice.'

He was about to head for the kitchen when he stopped.

'And do you think you could stop looking at me like that?' he said, exasperated.

'I — like what?'

'Like I've just crawled from beneath a stone,' Matthew said flatly. 'Ever since I agreed to go to this confounded party with Cassie, you've had disapproval in every inch of your face. Why?'

That was exactly the word Cassie had used. Helen didn't disapprove exactly, she just didn't like the arrangement. And the only reason she had was jealousy. Pure and simple jealousy.

'It's not up to me to approve or disapprove,' she said awkwardly. 'I just don't think much good will come of it.'

'Why?'

The frank question shook her and she was already blushing.

'Well — because, as you've seen tonight, Cassie's still involved with Ian.'

'It was a party, Helen,' Matthew said. 'A one-off thing.'

And what about that kiss? Had that been a one-off thing? But Helen didn't say anything.

'Helen,' Matthew began patiently, 'I can go out with Cassie and both of us know there are no strings attached. As you say, she's still involved with Ian. All she wants is company.'

'Perhaps,' Helen conceded.

'There's no perhaps about it. But there's more to it than that,' he went on. 'Kerry has to learn that I have a life to live, and I have to learn to live that life.'

Helen knew he was thinking of his wife. In this room, it was impossible not to. The laughing eyes of beautiful Jenny Anderson had followed her from the silver photo frame all evening.

'It's really none of my business, Matthew.'

She might not have spoken for the notice he took.

'Cassie is uncomplicated, Helen. People know where they stand with her.'

'That's Cassie,' Helen agreed, trying to lighten the atmosphere.

Matthew gazed at her for a long time and the atmosphere was anything but light.

'If you and I went out for the evening,' he said at last, 'that would be an entirely different matter.'

'I really don't see — '

'You'd read far too much into it, Helen. Just as you're reading far too much into this evening.' If he saw how uncomfortable the conversation was making her feel, he paid no attention. 'But it's not just you. It's me, too. I've been in love. I've been married.' His gaze rested briefly on the silver photo frame. 'I'm over losing Jenny,' he said, 'but I'm in no rush to get involved.'

He stepped forward and took her hand in his.

'For Cassie and me this was just a light-hearted evening out. She's like a kid sister. But if you and I went out, it would be very different. Wouldn't it?'

'I — I don't know.'

He gazed down at the hand trapped in his, and then looked into her face.

'I think you do, Helen.'

'I really think I ought to go, Matthew.'

'No.' He smiled. 'I'm not making a very good job of this, am I? I just wanted you to know that my taking Cassie out has nothing to do with the way I feel about you. I value your friendship very much. Since Jenny — well, I've haven't known anyone I could talk to as I can you.'

'I value your friendship, too.' Helen's voice was little more than a whisper.

'Good,' Matthew said. 'Then you can have some coffee and stop scowling at me.'

The gentle teasing brought forth a laugh and — afterwards, Helen was never quite sure how it happened. Did he make the first move? Or did she? Suddenly she was in his arms.

Perhaps he'd intended to give her a brotherly kiss and it went out of control. Perhaps she'd been so startled that her hands had gone instinctively to his shoulders. Helen just knew she didn't want to draw away, didn't want the kiss to end . . .

When it did, Matthew reached out his hand, but then snatched it back and strode away from her.

'I'll make the coffee,' he said, over his shoulder. 'I'm starving, too. The food tonight would have been good if it hadn't come in polite, bite-sized portions. Did you have time to look at the garden before it got dark? I'm quite proud of it. Jack Gibbs is doing a great job . . . '

He was talking for the sake of it, but he couldn't stop himself.

He wasn't sure what had happened. One minute he'd been telling her that he wasn't looking for involvement, and the next they'd been kissing . . .

When he carried the coffee into the sitting-room, Helen jumped.

The coffee was too hot to drink but, as normal conversation seemed impossible, they suffered in silence.

Long after Helen had gone home, Matthew

lay in bed and decided that one way and another, it had been a night he would prefer to forget.

The following day promised to be no better.

The telephone rang before he'd even sorted out their breakfast. Kerry answered it, and as he heard her chatting to their caller, his heart sank.

'It's Grandma,' Kerry told him, delighted. 'She's coming to stay with us.'

'What!' Matthew took the phone from her. 'Hello, Mum. What's this I hear about a visit?'

'Your father's spending a week in Germany,' she explained, 'so I thought I'd have a week with you. As it's such a long drive, I'll take the train. Can you can meet me on Tuesday, or shall I arrange a taxi?'

'Well, yes, I can meet you.' Matthew felt as if he were attempting to stop a steam-roller. 'The thing is — much as we'd love to see you, I'm up to my eyes in work at the moment. And Kerry will be at school all day.'

'Don't worry about me, darling,' she replied easily. 'I can amuse myself during the day, and when Kerry's home, I'll keep her amused so that you can get some work done.'

'It's a nice idea, Mum.' Matthew ran his hand through his hair. It was an appalling idea. 'But there isn't much for you to do here. Perhaps it would be better to wait until Dad can come. A weekend, perhaps.'

'There's plenty to do,' she told him with a laugh. 'I shan't be bored. You know me, Matthew.'

That was what worried him. Everything in the house would be wrong. And it would all be blamed on the lack of female influence in their lives.

'I'm already packed,' his mother added, and Matthew had to give in gracefully.

'Isn't it exciting?' Kerry said.

'Yes,' Matthew agreed.

As he got their breakfast, he made a mental note to re-stock the cupboards. Anything that smacked of convenience was out . . .

'Daddy?'

'Yes, sweetheart?'

'Can Amy come to tea tomorrow?'

Amy was Kerry's best friend, a nice girl with long, dark plaits and a tendency to shyness.

'So long as her mother says she can.'

'She hasn't got one,' Kerry replied in a matter-of-fact voice. 'Not a proper one. She's got a — a stairmummy.'

'A what? Oh!' Matthew laughed. 'I think you mean a stepmother.'

'That's it,' Kerry agreed. 'Amy likes her.'

'Then we'll ask her if Amy can come to tea.'

Kerry concentrated on her toast and marmalade for a few moments.

'Daddy? I'd like one of those. A step-mummy.'

That was surprising. But he supposed that until she'd heard about Amy's stepmother, Kerry hadn't realised that such people existed.

'It's not quite as simple as that,' Matthew told her.

'Why not? Amy's got one. Why can't I have one?'

'Because,' Matthew began slowly, 'for you to have a step-mother, I'd have to marry someone else. And it would have to be someone special, wouldn't it? Someone as special as your mummy.'

'Yes,' Kerry agreed, clearly seeing no problem there.

'Well, I've never met anyone else who's that special.'

'Miss Richards is special,' Kerry said.

'I'm sure she is, darling.' Miss Richards, Kerry's much-loved teacher, was approaching sixty.

'Now, eat your breakfast,' Matthew said, changing the subject. 'Helen said you could go and see the kittens this morning.'

'And Helen's special.'

When Matthew didn't comment, Kerry stared at him.

'Well, she is. Isn't she?'

'Of course Helen's special. So have you decided which kitten you're having? The black one, is it?'

Having successfully diverted Kerry's attention, Matthew breathed a sigh of relief.

When the subject of stepmothers was next raised, Matthew only hoped it wouldn't be during his mother's visit. Mum would be only too delighted to round up a dozen likely candidates for the post . . .

★ ★ ★

'What do you think, Sarah?' Alex asked.

'I think it looks reasonable,' Sarah answered truthfully.

For the last hour, she, Linda and Alex had been going through his calculations for the golf club tender with a fine-tooth comb.

Alex knew the way Tom worked, and how much was needed in the way of materials and manpower. Linda had typed out countless tenders and filed away as many calculations. And Sarah, knowing that she alone was responsible, was trying to envisage the job from the start to finish.

'If Tom was here,' Alex remarked, 'he could give us a figure off the top of his head. And it would be within a hundred pounds.'

'But he isn't,' Sarah said wearily. 'And his calculations aren't much help. I mean, look at this.' She nodded at the list of figures she was holding for a job they'd done last year. 'Other costs, eleven hundred pounds. What does he mean by 'other costs'?'

Alex looked at the figures.

'Vehicles? Travelling time? It's hard to say. Tom would have known though.'

Yes, Tom would have known.

For all Sarah knew, their tender could be laughable. But between them, they must have thought of everything.

'It's late,' she said. 'Type it up in the morning, Linda. I'll be in by ten and I'll deliver it by hand. I'd hate it to go astray in the post.'

They all knew what she really meant. She wasn't giving Gerald Compton a chance to 'lose' it conveniently.

'I'm sure it's fine, Alex,' she added, trying to boost his confidence.

'I hope so,' he murmured. 'How long do you think it'll be before we know?'

'If we don't get the work, I'm sure Gerald Compton will find a way of getting the news to us quickly. And if we do get it,' she added with a rueful smile, 'I'm equally sure we'll be the last to know.' She stood up.

'Still, there's no point in worrying. Either way, we'll know soon enough. By the way, Alex, have you had chance to speak to Lambert's?'

'I have,' he told her, 'and they want us to start as soon as possible. It's peanuts, of course, but it all helps, I suppose.'

'Do they want a quote?' Linda asked.

'No.' Doing a fair imitation of the softly-spoken Jim Lambert, he added, 'Lyndhurst's have always done me proud. I know I'll be getting a good job at a fair price.'

Sarah laughed.

'That's what I like to hear. Right, I'll see you both in the morning.'

She drove straight to the hospital. She knew every bump in the road, which was just as well, because she found it hard to concentrate on her driving.

Helen was sitting with her father. Sarah bent to kiss her before leaning over and kissing Tom's forehead.

She'd been coming to the hospital for so long that it felt like a second home; but it still shocked her to see Tom looking so frighteningly pale.

'You look all in,' Helen remarked with an anxious frown.

'I've had a hectic day.' Sarah smiled. 'But I'm OK.'

In truth, she felt jaded, and old. Ready for the scrap-heap.

'I'd better go,' Helen said. 'I told Melanie I'd call in. I've bought her a book.'

She fished in her canvas bag and showed Sarah the book of knitting patterns.

'What a lovely book.' Sarah thumbed through it. 'I wish I had time to try a few of these. Melanie will love it, I'm sure she will. This should tempt her into action.

'Give her my love, won't you? And tell her I'll call round in the afternoon.'

'I'll tell her,' Helen promised. 'See you later.'

When Helen left, Sarah pulled the chair closer to the bed, and held Tom's hand. Just being able to do that seemed to give her the strength to carry on.

She began talking, hoping as always that something she said would reach him.

She talked about the weather and how they needed rain for the garden. Then she told him about the kittens' antics, and how Kerry couldn't wait until her own kitten was old enough to leave its mother.

'Matthew's mother is staying with them,' she said. 'I gather that Matthew's as enthusiastic about it as you used to be when my mother visited. Kerry's thrilled, of course. She's getting spoiled to death. She's a lovely child. And she's longing for you to come home. We all are, Tom. I often think — '

Sometimes, the bright, inane chatter became impossible.

'Oh, Tom. I miss you so much.' Her heart leapt. 'Tom?'

The hand she held was quite still again, and Sarah tried to convince herself that she'd imagined that brief, heart-stopping movement of his fingers.

'Tom — please come back to me.' Her voice broke. 'I need you. I love you.'

Sarah put her hand against his face, and her touch was rewarded by a barely audible sigh, just before Tom opened his eyes.

Through a sudden blur of tears, Sarah looked into the eyes she had loved for as long as she could remember.

6

'Sarah?'

Sarah wouldn't have recognised her husband's voice, but he recognised her. Surely that meant he was going to be all right.

'Yes, it's me, darling.'

'What are you doing here?' Tom was becoming agitated. 'You shouldn't be here!'

'Of course your wife should be here, Tom.'

Sarah hadn't heard Dr Patrick come in. She supposed the nurse must have called him.

'How are you feeling, Tom?' he asked briskly. 'A little groggy, I imagine?'

'Did I ask — ' Tom's confused gaze didn't leave Sarah's face. 'Did I ask you to marry me?'

Sarah just managed to stop herself crying out.

'And you said yes?' Tom murmured, his eyes closing again.

'Tom?' Sarah wanted to shake him back to consciousness. 'Tom!'

Dr Patrick touched Sarah's arm.

'We'll have a chat in my office.'

He spoke to the nurse, and then led Sarah away.

'Sit down, Sarah.' he said, pulling forward a chair.

Sarah was too shaken to do anything else.

'I'm very encouraged,' the doctor said.

'Encouraged?' Sarah gazed at him.

'Yes,' the doctor confirmed. 'He recognised you immediately, and his speech was good.'

'But he didn't even know we were married! He's lost thirty years of his life. What about our children? He's not going to know them, is he?'

There was a light tap on the door, and a nurse came in with tea. Sarah murmured her thanks, and took a sip, knowing from experience that it would be lukewarm and sickly sweet. She was on first name terms with most of the nurses now, yet they couldn't remember that she didn't take sugar.

'Have you never wakened and not known where you are?' the doctor went on when they were alone.

'Well, yes.' Sarah had lost count of the mornings recently when she'd wakened. reached out for Tom and wondered where he was, before it all came rushing back to her. 'But that's a momentary thing, surely.'

'Usually,' he agreed. 'If you have a hangover, it takes a while longer for your thoughts to find some sort of order. And if your system is heavily drugged, like Tom's, it takes much longer to get your bearings.'

Sarah tried to accept what he was saying.

'We have a deal, Sarah. Remember?'

The doctor's voice was soothing, somehow, and Sarah nodded. She had promised to respect his judgement, and he had promised to be completely honest at all times.

'And you really are encouraged?' she asked.

'Very.' His smile was suddenly teasing. 'It must have been some proposal.'

'He never did ask me to marry him,' Sarah admitted with a shaky laugh. 'He tried, every day for about three weeks. In the end I told him that my answer was yes, because if we waited for him to propose, we'd die of old age before we walked down the aisle.'

Doctor Patrick chuckled, but then he was serious again. 'I never said it would be easy.'

'I know,' Sarah acknowledged. 'It's just that I expected — '

She didn't know what she'd expected. When Tom had said her name, she'd been filled with joy. But the fact that he didn't know where he was, or even what year it was, panicked her.

'I'll go and sit with him,' she said.

'Yes. And try to relax, Sarah. We've got something to build on, at last. Don't be alarmed when next he comes round — just use your common-sense.'

As Sarah sat by Tom's bed, holding his hand, she felt so much better than before. To hear his voice again had been wonderful.

During the next hour, three doctors stopped to examine him, and the nurse had stepped up her observations.

It was relatively quiet when Tom opened his eyes again.

'You shouldn't be here.'

'Why not?' Sarah asked, trying to keep her voice steady and reassuring.

He looked at her, puzzled.

'Where exactly are we, Tom?'

His gaze wandered to the hand that was holding his, and then rested on her face. Then his eyelids drooped, and Sarah thought he was sleeping again.

After a soft sigh, he said quietly, 'Hanged if I know, Sarah.'

The words were so unexpected, and the expression so typical of Tom, that Sarah's sudden laugh had her choking back a sob. 'I love you so much, Tom Lyndhurst.'

He didn't reply, but Sarah felt his fingers tighten around her own.

★ ★ ★

132

It was after ten o'clock next morning when Helen arrived at the shop.

Joe was always telling her to take things easy and come in late, but she never had, until today. For a moment, he was pleased that she'd taken his advice at last, but his pleasure was short-lived. Something was terribly wrong.

She looked terribly frail, as if she might snap in two. She was so pale, and her cheeks looked hollow.

'Helen?'

' 'Morning, Joe.'

'What's wrong? Your father — ' Joe hardly dared to ask.

She gave him a tight smile.

'No, nothing's wrong. In fact, it's good news. Dad came round last night, and I've actually spoken to him this morning. He's very weak, still drifting in and out of consciousness, but — '

She couldn't go on. She covered her face with her hands as if to hide the tears.

'Helen — ' Joe put his arms around her, and with a choked cry, she buried her face against him and clung to him as if she would never let him go.

Seconds drifted into minutes. He stroked her hair, murmuring soothing words, and slowly, her trembling ceased.

'How ridiculous,' she said on a shaky breath. 'I come here bearing good news and I can't stop crying.'

'You were so busy preparing yourself for bad news,' Joe said gently, 'you forgot to prepare yourself for the good.'

Helen lifted her head, dried her face with her hands, and gave him a watery smile.

'I expect you're right.'

'Of course I'm right. And I'm so pleased about your father.'

'There's still a long way to go but yes, it's good news.' Her smile was genuine now. 'It was the waiting that was so unbearable.'

Joe had seen that for himself.

'Thanks, Joe,' Helen said softly. 'For everything. For being so understanding. For doing your share of the work as well as mine . . . for listening, for caring.'

'Helen, there's nothing I wouldn't do for you.'

Her eyes were startled, and Joe wished he'd kept his thoughts to himself, as he'd meant to.

The last thing he'd wanted was to push her into something she wasn't ready for. He'd intended to wait until the time was right before he made his feelings known. And this wasn't the right time.

'You must know how I feel about you.' he said at last.

'Yes. I know.'

Helen had known for weeks, she realised. She'd tried to deny it, but she knew how he felt.

'I've tried not to think about it,' she admitted.

'That bad?' He attempted a joke.

'No,' Helen assured him with a smile. 'You're the best friend I could ever want.'

He grimaced.

'But?'

'There isn't a but, silly, and to prove it, as there seems to be something to celebrate, we'll go somewhere special this week. My treat.'

Just as Joe was telling himself that there must still be a 'but', Helen reached up and kissed him.

'Thanks, Joe. For giving me time to decide what I want.'

He swallowed.

'And do you know what you want?'

'Yes. I think so.' She was blushing. 'But for now, I'd like a cup of coffee. And then if you wouldn't mind dealing with the customers . . . ?'

'No. I mean, yes.'

Joe was still trying to grasp the meaning behind her smile.

'It's no good me serving anyone,' Helen went on lightly. 'I'm likely to burst into tears if anyone so much as mentions Dad.'

She went into the back room to make coffee, and Joe stood stock still, his heart thumping erratically. Helen knew what she wanted, and if he wasn't very much mistaken — was it possible that she could want him?

He didn't hear the bell when the shop door opened. It was only the polite cough that had him spinning round, with a huge smile on his face, to serve their customer.

★   ★   ★

A week later, Helen had just decided that her life was like the weather — all sunshine and clear skies — when a black cloud rolled in to spoil everything.

The day began well. She'd visited her father, who was looking better as each day passed, then called on her younger sister.

Melanie really was doing her best. She was resting, she was knitting and she wasn't complaining. And yet she still wasn't looking well.

Helen supposed that some women sailed through their pregnancies, and some didn't.

136

Unfortunately, Melanie didn't.

'Are you going out with Joe again tonight?' Melanie asked.

'Yes. Philip Blake, one of our customers, is into amateur dramatics. They're doing 'An Inspector Calls', and he gave us tickets.'

'You're a real couple now, aren't you?'

A real couple. Helen liked the sound of that.

'Yes, I suppose we are.'

'What about Matthew and Cassie?' Melanie asked. 'Are they a couple?'

'I don't know,' Helen replied briskly. Now that she knew how Joe felt about her, her embarrassment at that little scene, the night Matthew and Cassie had gone out together, no longer seemed important.

'Cassie's gone to Edinburgh with him today, hasn't she?'

Helen nodded.

'Matthew had to go on business, something to do with this book he's working on, and I suppose Cassie felt like a day out. I don't think it means anything.'

Melanie disagreed. 'Cassie seems keen. When I saw her, every sentence began with Matt says and Matt thinks.'

'But if Ian came back — Oh, who knows? Look, I'd better go.'

'Why not come round for a meal one

night? You and Joe?'

Helen laughed, happy to change the subject.

'Because you're supposed to be taking things easy, that's why.'

'I am taking things easy. I don't mean anything grand — Paul could get a take-away. I thought it would be nice, a foursome.'

'It would,' Helen agreed quickly. 'I'll give you a ring tomorrow and we'll fix something up.'

'Thanks for coming, Helen.'

Helen gave her a quick hug. Suddenly, she felt closer to her sister than she had for years.

She drove home, looking forward to a long bath before going to the theatre with Joe, but from then on, everything went wrong.

She'd been in the house less than two minutes when the phone rang.

'Helen? I'm sorry to bother you . . . '

Helen recognised the soft, refined voice immediately. It was Matthew's mother — 'please call me Marcie'.

'I wondered if you could spare a few minutes?' she said.

'Of course,' Helen replied immediately. 'Is there a problem?'

'It's Kerry, I'm afraid. She took a fall in the playground today.'

'Oh no!'

'She's all right,' Marcie assured her quickly. 'She's feeling a bit sorry for herself though and I wondered if you could come over — perhaps try and cheer her up.'

'Yes, of course.'

Helen rushed out of the house, wondering exactly what Marcie expected her to do. Kerry doted on her grandmother. If Marcie couldn't cheer her up, Helen didn't think she'd be any more successful.

Helen knocked on the Andersons' door and let herself in. A very tearful Kerry threw herself into her arms, and sobbed out the whole story.

'I can't bend my arm. And Daddy's not here.' She showed Helen the enormous sticking plaster that covered her elbow.

'He's gone to Edinburgh,' Helen said lightly.

'They took an X-ray,' Marcie explained, 'just as a precaution.'

'I expect she'll feel better when her father gets back,' Helen said.

Helen was sure she would. Despite Matthew's clucking, Kerry was growing into a tomboy. Normally, she took the bumps and bruises in her stride, but today she wanted a hug from her father, and he wasn't there.

Helen was surprised Marcie couldn't cope.

She always looked to be in control of everything.

Helen took Marcie and Kerry home to see the kittens, which passed an hour or so, then went back and read a story to Kerry, but as soon as Helen suggested she should leave, the tears started again.

As the minutes ticked by, Helen saw the theatre slipping from her grasp. For some reason, Kerry was particularly unhappy, and Helen knew that if she went out she'd spend the entire evening worrying about the little girl.

'I'll see if I can ring, Joe,' she said at last.

'Kerry,' Marcie coaxed. 'We can't let Helen ruin her evening, can we?'

'It's all right,' Helen told her. 'Joe will understand.'

Marcie insisted that Helen use their telephone and without sounding rude, it was impossible to refuse. It had to be said though that Marcie had an inquisitive streak that bordered on plain nosey.

As Helen had guessed, Joe hadn't left. She told him about Kerry's fall.

'Do you think we'll be able to get tickets for another evening?'

'I gained the impression that we could walk in and choose whichever seats we wanted.' The question amused him.

'Or perhaps you'd rather take someone else,' Helen said.

'Now there's a thought,' he replied gravely. 'I'll see if Cindy Crawford's free.'

Helen laughed.

'On the off-chance she's busy,' Joe added, 'I'll get tickets for another night. Tomorrow OK?'

'Lovely.' Helen's heart filled with a sudden warmth. 'I knew you'd understand, Joe.'

When Helen replaced the receiver, the phone rang immediately.

'I'll get it,' Kerry said, running towards it.

Helen was grateful. She didn't want to talk to Matthew.

But it was Kerry's young friend, Amy.

'The phone bills that pair run up,' Marcie said with an exasperated laugh. 'They see each other every day, so heaven knows what they find to talk about.'

While Kerry updated Amy on the day's events, and told her that 'my friend Helen's staying until Daddy gets home', Helen and Marcie had a cup of tea.

In the nicest possible way, Marcie soon had Helen's life story.

'You're a big hit with Kerry,' Marcie told her.

'She's a lovely child.'

'She is.' Marcie sighed. 'It's a shame that

— still, we have to make the most of it. don't we?'

'Matthew copes very well. And Kerry's happy.'

'I know,' Marcie agreed. 'But it's been four years now. I thought Matthew might have — I feel that Kerry needs a woman in her life.' She brightened suddenly. 'I suppose there's plenty of time, though.'

Don't hold your breath, Helen thought. Matthew had told her in no uncertain terms that he wasn't looking for involvement . . .

Much to their amazement, Kerry was eventually persuaded to go to bed. She was worn out but she fought against sleep as Helen read from 'Alice in Wonderland'.

'Helen?'

'Yes?'

'When will Daddy be home?'

Kerry had asked the same question at least a dozen times and each time, Helen gave the same answer.

'I don't know, love. It's a long way, so it might be late.'

'It's not fair.' Kerry's chin wobbled and her eyes filled with tears.

'Your daddy has to work,' Helen said gently. 'And you're lucky, Kerry. Most daddies go to an office to work, but yours works at home.'

'It's still not fair,' Kerry grumbled.

'Go to sleep.' Helen suggested gently. 'Then, when you wake up, Daddy will be home.'

When Kerry eventually fell asleep, there were still tears on her lashes.

Had Matthew and Cassie stopped for dinner somewhere? Were they laughing together?

Kerry was five years old, and entitled to childish behaviour. Helen wasn't, but she still couldn't help thinking that it was indeed unfair. Matthew should be there when his daughter needed him, not enjoying himself with Cassie.

She pushed her thoughts aside and went downstairs.

'She's asleep. I can't see her waking before morning, so I'll go now.'

'Oh!' Marcie seemed dismayed. 'Oh dear. I was rather hoping you'd stay until Matthew got back.'

'But — '

'You're right.' Marcie took a deep breath. 'You've done more than enough for us, and I'm being selfish. I was going to take a sleeping pill and go to bed, but of course, I can't do that, in case Kerry wakes. Never mind, you go, dear.'

Helen knew she couldn't refuse.

'You go to bed, Marcie. I'll stay until Matthew gets back.'

'Will you, dear?' Marcie brightened immediately. 'I'm sure he won't be long.'

Marcie was soon in bed. Sitting there on her own, Helen tried not to think about Matthew and Cassie, but it was difficult. Business was one thing — she wouldn't have minded helping out then — but giving up her evening so that Matthew could entertain her sister was another thing altogether.

Had Melanie been right when she'd called their sister and Matthew 'a real couple'? I don't care, Helen told herself again. But she did care, and the more she thought about it, the angrier she became. And no wonder!

Unlike Cassie, she wasn't acceptable for nights out with Matthew. Oh no, she would read too much into it, he'd said. But when it came to sitting in his house, bored stiff, her evening ruined — that was fine. Helen Doormat Lyndhurst!

When Matthew's car pulled up outside, Helen gave herself a sharp talking to. She would be polite — and then she would leave.

In the eleven and a half minutes it took him to say goodnight to Cassie and walk the ten yards to his door, her temper reached breaking point.

She met him in the hall. His jacket was

144

slung over his shoulder and his tie was hanging out of the pocket. Very businesslike, Helen thought grimly.

'Helen — what the devil are you doing here?'

Helen could have hit him. Then she spotted the alarm in his eyes.

'Kerry's fine,' she assured him quickly. 'She's upstairs fast asleep. She fell over in the playground — '

But Matthew was taking the stairs two at a time. She supposed he was entitled to some sort of explanation, so she waited in the sitting-room. She didn't have long to wait.

'She's asleep,' he said. 'What did you say happened?'

Helen told him.

'She's perfectly all right. If you'd been here, she would have had a few tears and forgotten all about it. She missed you a lot.'

Some of Matthew's colour had returned but he was puzzled.

'I still don't see why you're here.'

'Your mother couldn't cope. Kerry was upset. She didn't like the idea of you gallivanting around the countryside when — '

'Gallivanting?' he interrupted softly. 'That's a big word for a five-year-old. Do I detect disapproval — again?'

'How you run your life is your affair,'

145

Helen replied airily. 'But while you were — '

'Gallivanting around the countryside?'

'While you were doing that, your mother was reaching the end of her tether. She took a sleeping pill and went to bed.'

'A sleeping pill?' His laugh was disbelieving. 'Now I've heard it all!'

'You're right, Matthew,' Helen snapped. 'It's all lies. I engineered the whole thing. I pushed Kerry over in the playground, gave up my plans for the evening, just so that I could spend a few minutes in your sparkling company. Isn't that what all the women do? After all, you're God's gift to the female race. Or think you are!' She turned on her heel. 'Goodnight!'

'Helen, what the — '

Helen rounded on him.

'It might take eleven and a half minutes to say goodnight to Cassie, but not me. Goodnight, Matthew!'

She tried to slam the door, but he was in the way. He somehow pulled her back inside, closed the door and stood with his back to it.

'If you're interested,' he said at last, 'it took eleven minutes twenty seconds to transfer Cassie's shopping from my car to your house. Your sister's addicted to shopping.'

Helen almost smiled at that, but she knew that if she did, the tears would follow.

The future was hers for the taking. She had a dream — herself and Joe in a small cottage in the country, roses round the door, children in the garden . . . But Matthew — the mere thought of him — pushed that dream just out of reach.

He lifted her chin and forced her to look at him through tear-bright eyes.

'I wasn't expecting gratitude,' she managed to say, 'but neither was I expecting 'what the devil are you doing here?' '

'I'm sorry.' Matthew took his hand away. 'But seeing you here gave me the fright of my life. I thought you were about to break the bad news to me. Anyway, I'm sorry your evening was ruined,' he added. 'If I'd known, I would have got back sooner.'

'It wasn't important.' His apology made her feel like a five-year-old.

'Something's important!'

'I was tired,' Helen lied, 'and annoyed at missing my night at the theatre. I over-reacted.'

'Hmm. We seem to make a habit of over-reacting.'

She didn't have an answer to that.

'I thought we were friends, Helen.'

Helen knew exactly what he meant. They had been friends, but everything had changed the night he took Cassie to the party.

'Of course we're friends.' She gave him a bright smile. 'We'll forget tonight, pretend it never happened.'

'No we won't. It'll come between us — just as that other night's come between us.'

The silence between them was filled with heavy memories of that other night.

'Greg Saunders, the chap I saw today, is an old friend,' Matthew said at last. 'We met when I was at university.'

The sudden change of subject confused Helen, but she was grateful for it.

'He and his wife have invited me to spend the day with them, the Sunday after next. And Kerry, of course.'

Helen didn't have a clue what he was getting at. Had she made such a fuss that he now intended to warn her whenever he was taking Cassie out?

'Will you come with us?'

Helen's head flew up. 'Sorry?'

'I wondered if you'd like to come with us,' Matthew said calmly. 'I mentioned you, and you were included in the invitation. I think you'd like Jean and Greg.'

Why had he mentioned her to his friends? Why wasn't he afraid that she'd read too much into it?

'I suppose you want someone to take care of Kerry?'

'No. Greg and Jean have two children of their own. I'm sure the three of them will amuse themselves.'

Helen tried to read his expression, but she couldn't. 'Then why me?'

'Because I don't like living like this, Helen. Every time we meet, we always end up trying to pretend it never happened!' Matthew said. 'I want us to be friends again and I thought it would be nice if we could spend some time together. Besides,' he added with a smile, 'it will be quite a novelty to come home and know you're not waiting for me like an irate parent!'

Helen laughed, and her rural idyll with Joe slipped further into the distance.

'Will you come with us?' Matthew asked.

'Yes.'

The quick acceptance surprised him.

'Thank you.'

Helen wondered if she really liked Matthew, or whether his good looks were the only attraction. When all was said and done, she didn't know him terribly well. And yet . . .

What would Cassie say when she found out? And what on earth would Joe say?

★　★　★

Sarah was about to leave the house when Matthew and Kerry called.

'We've brought these for Uncle Tom,' Kerry explained, handing over the most perfect white roses Sarah had ever seen.

'Kerry, they're beautiful.' Sarah hugged the little girl. 'He'll be so pleased.'

'Can we go and see him soon?' Kerry asked.

'Soon,' Sarah agreed.

Sarah didn't know what Kerry would make of her 'Uncle Tom'. He wasn't the laughing giant of a man she'd known before the accident. He was making excellent progress, everyone said so, but he tired very easily, and sometimes he seemed almost distant.

On the other hand, perhaps Kerry's cheerful chatter would be what he needed. Tom hated being fussed over, and Sarah suspected that, between them, the family were driving him mad.

'How about next week?' she suggested. 'I'll see what the doctors say. They won't let Tom get tired.'

'I won't let him,' Kerry promised eagerly.

'It would just be for a few minutes,' Matthew warned her. 'And you wouldn't have to talk non-stop.'

Kerry looked appalled at the very idea of

her doing such a thing and Sarah chuckled to herself.

'He'd love to see you, Kerry,' she said.

Delighted at the prospect, Kerry proceeded to talk non-stop.

'We're having a day out on Sunday,' she told Sarah. 'And Helen's coming with us.'

'Yes, I know.' Sarah wished she could sound more enthusiastic.

She and Tom had worried that Helen might never marry, which would be a shame as she had so much to give.

When Helen had started seeing Joe, Sarah couldn't have been more pleased. Joe was perfect for Helen. But Joe was completely different to Matthew. Joe was younger, less intense. He didn't have a daughter, or memories of a woman he'd once loved. Joe wouldn't break Helen's heart.

Sarah wanted to tell herself that there was nothing in it, but Helen's reticence on the subject spoke volumes.

She caught Matthew's gaze on her.

'Cassie and Helen are very different, Matthew.'

'Very,' he agreed calmly.

If Helen had been sixteen, Sarah would have forbidden her to see Matthew, but her eldest daughter was a grown woman who had to make her own mistakes. Sarah only hoped

151

that those mistakes wouldn't bring heartache on a scale that Helen had never dreamed of . . .

The phone rang and Sarah went to answer it.

'Gerald Compton's been on the phone,' Tom's secretary, Linda, greeted her. 'I told him you'd call him back. I thought you might want advance warning.'

Not today! Sarah groaned silently.

'Thanks, Linda.'

'You think it's bad news?'

'Would he ring us if it's good?' Sarah tried not to sound too worried. 'I would have expected a letter. I'll ring him as soon as I can, then I'll let you know.'

Putting off the dreadful moment, Sarah kept Matthew and Kerry talking for as long as possible.

When they'd gone, she tapped out the golf club number. She prayed it was good news. Tom had only asked about the business once, and she'd told him everything was fine. Until she had something positive to tell him, that was the way she wanted to keep it.

The phone was answered almost immediately by Gerald Compton.

'I have some good news for you,' he said, and Sarah's blood ran cold.

He was enjoying this far too much. He

might have news for her, but she couldn't imagine it being good.

'Oh?'

'Indeed. The committee has voted unanimously to give Lyndhurst's the contract.'

He waited for a reaction from Sarah.

'That *is* good news,' Sarah said at last, wondering why she had never felt less like celebrating in her life.

'For us, too,' Gerald Compton agreed. 'Your tender was — ' There was amusement in his voice. 'Er — very competitive.'

Sarah closed her eyes tight. What he meant was that their tender was ridiculous. They must have miscalculated, forgotten something.

They'd have to undertake this large contract for an impossibly low price, and Tom's business would be finished . . .

7

'The contract stated minimal disruption for staff and club members, Sarah.' Gerald Compton nodded towards the three Lyndhurst vehicles in the golf club car-park. 'It's not good enough.'

Sarah glanced at the two vans and a lorry, all proudly displaying the Lyndhurst name.

'It's hardly disruptive,' she murmured.

Unfortunately, the lorry was parked in the club president's space, and one of the vans was hiding a name-board for 'G Compton — Secretary'.

Sarah looked about at an almost deserted car-park that would comfortably hold a hundred cars.

'It might have been more disruptive,' she pointed out, 'if they'd parked further away and then carried materials the length of the car park.'

'But to choose the reserved spots!'

Sarah suspected the men had enjoyed a chuckle about that. Even so, it gave them the shortest and safest route to where they were working.

'And do you really need so many vehicles

here?' Gerald demanded.

'Yes!'

Obviously the lorry wouldn't be there on a regular basis, but short of parachuting the men in . . .

Sarah suppressed a smile. She had a mountain of worries, most of them centred around this job, and here she was arguing about the parking.

This was all too petty for words. Golfers, it seemed, were more than happy to tramp several miles across a golf course, but couldn't manage a couple of yards across the carpark.

But as they say, the customer is always right.

'I'll have a word with the men,' she promised, 'and make sure they only use these spaces when there's no alternative.'

'Do that, Sarah. And bear in mind that although the decision to give this work to Lyndhurst's was unanimous, it wasn't made lightly.'

'I'm sure it wasn't,' Sarah murmured. She could guess who had protested most loudly, too.

As if aware of her thoughts, he said, 'For your information, I argued your case.'

He allowed himself a small smile at Sarah's shocked expression, then went on grimly, 'It was a good competitive tender but several committee members expressed doubts. Without Tom, the firm's an unknown quantity. The thing that finally swayed it in your favour was Tom's reputation.'

Sarah didn't doubt it.

'Tom's worked hard for that reputation.' She gave a confident smile. 'And that includes making sure he has an excellent work force backing him.'

'Perhaps,' Gerald agreed doubtfully. 'But don't expect anyone to make allowances for Tom's absence — we can't afford to. This job has got to be up to standard. It must be finished on time and within the budget.'

'It will be. I guarantee it!' Sarah lifted her chin and met his cool gaze.

A car drove past, but he didn't look away. Finally, in a voice that was all the more chilling for its lack of bluster, he said, 'It had better be, Sarah. Because if it isn't, your business will be finished!'

★ ★ ★

After a day that had been far too hot for comfort, the evening air was refreshingly cool, perfect for a leisurely stroll home.

'Let's make a detour past the shop,' Helen suggested.

156

'You can't keep away, can you?' Joe teased.

'I'll have you know I was almost roasted alive doing that window display this afternoon.' Helen laughed. 'I'd like to see that the spotlights are actually on the books.' She glanced at him. 'You're not in a rush to get home, are you?'

'Of course not.' The question seemed to amuse him. Perhaps, like Helen, he was reluctant to end such a pleasant evening.

Much to her surprise, they'd had a highly enjoyable time with Melanie and Paul. Helen had felt it only fair to warn Joe that her young sister had a tendency to complain and Paul might bore him to death with his 'get-rich-quick' business schemes.

She'd been totally wrong. Melanie hadn't looked particularly well, but they hadn't heard a single complaint. She'd seemed contented and happy, and Paul had been too busy watching his wife to think about business.

They had both matured, Helen supposed, and she smiled to herself. They had certainly needed to.

'Perfect,' Joe announced, flourishing a hand at the show window. 'We'll have a queue a mile long in the morning.'

'We should be so lucky!'

All the same, Helen was proud as she gazed

at the bookshop. *First Editions* might not be the biggest business in the world, but it was all theirs.

As they walked on, she was deep in thought. Perhaps one day she and Joe would be entertaining Melanie and Paul in their country cottage . . . Perhaps Helen would be telling Melanie the names they'd chosen for their child . . .

Or perhaps her imagination was playing tricks. For all she knew, Joe might run a mile if he knew what she was thinking. He'd never actually mentioned the word love.

But then, he hadn't needed to. Helen knew without hearing the words . . .

'We ought to make the most of this weather.' Joe's voice broke into her thoughts. 'How about a day out on Sunday? We could drive out to the coast.'

The question took Helen completely by surprise.

'That would have been nice,' she murmured, 'but I can't. I've already agreed to go on a picnic with Matthew and Kerry.'

'I see.'

His voice was even and pleasant, as usual, and somehow that made her feel guilty which was absurd.

'I wasn't expecting you to suggest a day out,' she added.

Joe said nothing.

'You don't mind, do you, Joe?'

There was a brief pause.

'I don't have to mind, do I?'

Helen's heart sank.

'Matthew asked me along — well, Kerry doesn't get as many days out as she would if Matthew's wife was still alive. I expect he wants someone to help keep an eye on her.'

* * *

She was babbling, she knew. 'It's easier with two, isn't it? I expect that's all he wants, someone to help amuse Kerry. And perhaps he wants — '

'I don't care what *he* wants,' Joe cut her off sharply. 'It's what *you* want that concerns me.'

She stopped, staring at him. 'What I — ?'

'Yes, Helen. What do you want? Do you want Matthew? Heaven knows, you keep throwing yourself at him.'

'I do not throw myself at him!' she said, indignant.

'You do. If he clicks his fingers, you jump? Why? What exactly do you feel for him? Do you know?'

Joe gave her no time to consider the barrage of questions.

'Any fool can see he's not right for you. I think you just feel sorry for him and Kerry,' he added.

'What utter rubbish! It's not like that at all.'

'Then tell me what it *is* like!'

They had reached Helen's gate, and she was trying in vain to open it when Joe grabbed her arms and whirled her around to face him.

'For God's sake, Helen, what does it take to get through to you? I love you. I want to marry you.'

Helen tried to speak. She knew he was waiting for some reaction, but she was too shocked to utter a single word.

'You've got some serious thinking to do, Helen.' Joe dropped his arms to his sides. 'When you decide what it is you want, let me know.'

Still in shock, she clung to the gate and watched him walk back down the street without a backward glance.

★ ★ ★

Several members of the hotel staff had gone down with 'flu, so Cassie had been working nights. She'd learned long ago to take the many and varied disasters of reception work in her stride. but all the same, she was

160

pleased to leave the busy desk and step out into the brilliant sunshine.

She was crossing the car-park when her heart gave a sudden lurch. Ian was there.

She stopped and took a deep breath before walking towards him. Her heart slowed to a more bearable pace, and then she recalled the beautiful Julie — the strange girl she'd found completely at home in his London flat, helping to decorate it, wearing a shirt Cassie herself had given him . . .

'Hello, Ian.'

Her voice was cool. She was surprised to see him, of course, and not altogether pleased. She couldn't see him any longer as the boy she'd shared every secret with, or the man that she'd planned to spend the rest of her life with. All she saw was someone she'd once known. Not a stranger exactly, but certainly not Ian.

She couldn't help noticing how exhausted he looked. And he was much thinner . . .

'Is this yours?' she asked, nodding at the unfamiliar car. 'Business must be good.'

'The old one finally gave up the ghost.' He looked at her for long moments. 'I had to come, Cass. We need to talk.'

'I know.' His earnest, almost boyish expression touched her heart.

When they were sitting in the car, he made

no attempt to start the engine. They sat in what quickly became a nerve-wracking silence.

Ian's old Mini had been a temperamental heap of rust, but Cassie felt a sudden longing for its familiar, tatty upholstery.

'About that party at the hotel,' Ian said at last. 'I would have — I mean, I wish we could have talked that night.'

Cassie had tried to forget that awful night.

'You were with Matthew Anderson,' Ian remarked unnecessarily.

'Yes, I've been out with him several times. He's been a good friend to the family.' She glanced at him. Should she tell him how she was feeling? Yes . . . 'We've been through a lot while you've been in London. We didn't know if Dad would live, we didn't know if the business would survive. Matthew's been a good friend.'

Ian drowned her words by starting the car and driving out of the car-park.

Cassie tried several times to continue the conversation, but it seemed they'd lost the ability to talk about even the simplest of things.

He drove them out to the hill, one of their old haunts. Cassie wished he'd chosen some other spot, but there was nowhere round here that couldn't be described as

162

one of their old haunts.

When she turned to look at him, she saw again how awful he looked.

'You're tired,' she said quietly.

'Of course I'm tired. I've been driving all night!' His voice softened. 'I had to come and see you, Cass. We can't go on like this.'

'Nothing's right any more.'

'It could be, if only — '

He reached inside his jacket pocket, then stretched out his hand. Nestling in his palm was Cassie's engagement ring.

She stared at the ring that she'd worn for so long. Her happiness had known no limits when he had first put it on her finger. It had symbolised everything she had held most dear.

For the first few days after returning it, she'd felt strange without its reassuring weight on her hand.

'I carry it with me everywhere, Cass.' Ian's eyes were quietly pleading. 'I'd like to put it back where it belongs.'

Tears stung Cassie's eyes. She longed to throw her arms around his neck and forget everything.

She hadn't known a second's happiness since she'd thrown her ring back at him — but she'd lost a lot more than a ring. The damage had been done, and Cassie was no longer sure that they could put things right.

'I'm sorry, Ian' she whispered shakily. 'I just don't know what I want any more. Things change. People change.'

'People don't change,' Ian argued. 'The circumstances might have changed, but I certainly haven't. I've always hated it when we're apart. That's why I had to come this weekend.

'I miss you so much, Cass. We've got to sort this out.'

He saw the bewilderment in her eyes, and the desperate uncertainty.

'I haven't changed, Cass,' he insisted, taking her in his arms. 'I've loved you for years, and I always will love you.'

He lowered his head and kissed the tears that glistened on her lashes, then he kissed lips that were warm and so very familiar.

'You can't give up on us, Cass, just because we have to be apart at the moment. I won't let you.'

★   ★   ★

'Uncle Tom doesn't look very well,' Sarah warned little Kerry. 'He looks a bit funny, lying down, but he's just the same.'

Sarah had doubts about this visit, but Tom was as keen to see the child as Kerry was to see him, and the doctors thought the visit would do him good.

Holding Kerry's hand tightly, Sarah pushed open the door to Tom's room. To her surprise and pleasure, he was sitting upright, with a mound of pillows behind him.

'Uncle Tom!' Kerry wriggled free and skipped off to perch herself on the edge of Tom's bed. She handed him a small posy of flowers, carefully fastened with yellow ribbon. 'These are from our garden.'

'Thank you, Kerry.' Tom was deeply touched. 'And thank you for all the other flowers you've sent — and these lovely cards.'

These 'lovely cards', hand-made and brightly painted, were leaning in the window, and Kerry explained what each one was supposed to signify.

'If you look in this cupboard,' Tom said, 'you might find something nice.'

Kerry was on her knees, diving into the small bedside locker and finding a box of chocolates.

'For me?' she asked, thrilled.

'For you,' Tom replied gravely. 'But don't tell everyone, because then they'll want a box. Only my favourite visitors get one.'

Kerry hugged the box to her, went into raptures over the picture of the kittens on the lid, and gave Tom a big kiss.

'I wanted to see you before,' he told him, 'but they wouldn't let me.'

'Well, you're here now, that's the main thing.' Tom chuckled.

'I can only stay for five minutes though,' Kerry said, adding in a whisper, 'If I stay longer, you'll be ill again.' Her young forehead creased in thought. 'At least, I expect that's it.'

'We certainly don't want that to happen,' Tom said, trying to keep a straight face. 'As soon as your five minutes are up, I'll chase you out myself.'

'Uncle Tom!' Kerry shrieked with laughter. 'You'll get into terrible trouble if you get out of bed.'

Sarah laughed at the two of them. This light-hearted fooling around was just what Tom needed.

'Daddy's outside,' Kerry explained. 'He'll come and see you another day. They won't let too many people come at the same time.'

Kerry told Tom about the kittens, about her grandmother's visit, about the gardens, about the picnic she, Helen and Matthew were going on the next day, about her teacher, about her best friend . . .

Then Sarah saw he was looking tired.

'I think your five minutes were up quite a while ago, Kerry,' she suggested gently.

'I'll come again soon,' Kerry promised. 'I'm so glad you didn't die.'

'So am I,' Tom said, his eyes twinkling.

Sarah took the little girl back to Matthew and then returned to Tom's room.

'What a tonic that child is.' Tom smiled. 'Matthew's a very lucky man.'

'She's lovely,' Sarah agreed.

It seemed strange to think of a man who had lost his wife as lucky, but that was Tom, always able to look on the bright side.

'Are you all right, love?' she asked. 'Not too tired?'

'Sarah, when something's wrong, you'll be the first to know. OK?' He took her hand in his, and smiled to conceal his impatience. 'Stop worrying, woman. I'm not going anywhere.'

'I wasn't worrying,' Sarah lied. 'Kerry tires me out and she tires Matthew out. I don't see why you should be any different.'

'Of course I'm different.' Tom laughed softly. 'I've spent most of my life surrounded by chattering women. I'm immune.' He leaned forward to kiss her.

'Now, before I forget,' he went on, 'perhaps you'd ask Alex to call in and see me.'

'Alex?' Sarah frowned.

'Yes, Alex,' Tom said drily. 'Perhaps he'll

tell me what's happening at the yard while I'm stuck here.'

Sarah groaned inwardly. Tom never had been a good patient, and she didn't suppose he ever would be.

'I've told you what's happening,' she said quietly.

'You've told me everything's wonderful.'

'It is.'

'What jobs have we got? What are the men doing?' Tom was impatient.

'We've got several jobs,' Sarah informed him. 'And most of the men are busy at the golf club.'

'Doing what?' Tom demanded in amazement. 'There was nothing — ' He frowned. 'There was a big job up there I planned to tender for.'

Sarah nodded.

'That's the one. Except there's more work involved than there was when you discussed it with Gerald Compton. An unexpected planning decision went their way.'

'So who tendered? Alex? Good grief, Sarah, he's never done anything like that before. And why the devil wasn't I consulted?'

'Will you calm down? Honestly, you're supposed to be getting better not working yourself into a state.' Sarah took a long steadying breath. 'I'll say this once, Tom, and once only. Alex tendered. He hadn't done anything like that before, no, but he's spent long enough working beside you to know what he's doing. The tender was competitive — '

'How much?' Tom interrupted.

'The tender was competitive,' Sarah continued firmly.

It was, too. She knew that now. As soon as Gerald Compton had told her so, she'd rushed to tell Alex. She had also told Alex that they had received Gerald Compton's backing, too.

As Compton had said, the job had to be completed to a high standard, on time and within the budget. But she and Alex had rested a little easier with the knowledge that their tender had been a good one.

'The tender was accepted,' Sarah repeated, 'and work up there is going very well. The business is thriving.'

'But how much was our tender?'

'That's all I have to say, Tom,' Sarah said. 'At the moment, the business is no concern of yours. There's no need for you to know and I won't have you worrying about it.'

Tom's mouth dropped open.

'You're not going to tell me?'

'That's right, I'm not going to tell you. In fact, I refuse to discuss the business at all.'

'That is the most ridiculous thing — '

'And I'm not letting Alex within a hundred yards of this place,' Sarah cut him off. 'Doctor Patrick would have a fit if he thought you were fretting about the business.'

Tom was speechless.

'And don't think you can wheedle your way round the staff and get your own personal telephone,' she warned him, 'because I'll have a word with them about that, too!'

Sarah suspected that Tom was more dazed by her attitude than anything else. He'd never seen her like this, because she'd never been like this before. There had never been a need until now.

'The business doesn't need you exclusively,' Sarah told him. 'When all's said and done, it's only a means of making a living. But *I* need you, Tom. I need to wake up in the morning and know that you're there. The children need you, too. We want you home!'

'But I will be, Sarah. Soon. I'd be home now if they weren't so . . . pernickety.'

Sarah shook her head at this claim from a man too weak to get out of bed.

'When you're home,' she said sweetly, 'we can discuss the business. Until then, I have nothing more to say on the matter . . . '

★ ★ ★

While Kerry took Matthew off to fly her kite the following Sunday, Helen cleared away the remains of their picnic. Why was it, she wondered, that food tasted twice as good eaten in the fresh air?

She propped herself up on her elbow and watched their not very impressive attempts to get the kite launched. They had a vast expanse of beach before them, but there was little breeze.

Finally it was airborne but, after a few minutes, Kerry was bored. She came running over to Helen.

'I'm going to look for some shells. Uncle Tom said I was to take him one when I next visit him.'

'Don't go too far,' Matthew warned her. 'Just to that big rock over there.'

Kerry helped herself to an apple and set off in search of her shells, and Matthew flopped beside Helen.

'All days should be like this,' he remarked. 'Good food, good company and good weather.'

'I expected it to pour with rain,' Helen admitted with a smile. 'It always seems to at the weekend.'

She wondered how Joe was spending his day. The atmosphere at the shop had varied between tense and frosty recently. His parting

'Enjoy your picnic tomorrow' had left her unable to do anything but murmur her thanks.

The shop had been so busy that they'd barely had time to exchange more than a dozen words.

If Helen was honest she was secretly relieved. She had carried on involved telephone conversations and served customers with her mind echoing Joe's words. *'I love you. I want to marry you.'*

She heard those words when she tried to sleep, and she heard them again when she woke . . .

She pulled herself together. How long had she been sitting here lost in thought? Not that Matthew seemed to mind.

'Kerry tells me your mother's planning another visit,' she remarked.

'She is,' Matthew confirmed with a rueful smile. 'Fortunately, my father's coming with her. And fortunately, they can only stay one night.'

Helen laughed at his evident relief. 'She means well. She just wants you to — '

'Get married again,' Matthew finished for her.

'I was going to say that she wants you to be happy.'

Matthew gathered up a handful of sand.

'In her eyes, it's one and the same thing.'

A lot of people would agree with her, too, Helen thought, with Joe's words echoing in her mind again.

'I'm happy enough as I am,' Matthew said firmly.

'Are you?'

'Yes, I think so. I enjoy my work, my home and my friends, and I have Kerry. You can't really ask for more than that, can you?'

'It's more than a lot of people have.'

'And I certainly won't marry again just to please my mother,' he assured her with a smile. 'It's an enormous step to take.'

She suspected he was frightened of loving again because he couldn't bear the thought of losing again. And who could blame him?

'It was different with Jenny,' he said softly. 'The first time I saw her, I knew. It sounds corny, doesn't it? The proverbial look across the crowded room. But that's how it was.'

It did sound corny. It was all very well in novels, but very dubious in real life. She couldn't think of anyone else she knew who'd had that experience.

True, Melanie and Paul had fallen head over heels in a very short space of time, but even their whirlwind romance had been based on more than just one look.

Cassie and Ian's love had grown slowly,

after many years of friendship. And from what she'd been told, Mum had spent months fighting off her dad's advances before she grew to like him and finally to love him.

As for herself and Joe, Helen couldn't even remember the first time they met. Perhaps Joe could . . . she must ask him. There had been a group of people at university, all with similar interests, and she and Joe had become part of it.

She could remember discussing lectures with him over endless cups of coffee, and how he'd calmed her pre-exam jitters. And her pleasure at the rare letters they exchanged after university.

But for the life of her, she couldn't remember the moment when she saw him for the first time . . .

'Everyone loved Jenny,' Matthew's light voice went on. 'She was so full of life. She was bright, funny, beautiful. It's hard, even now, to accept that she's gone.'

'Kerry must be very like her,' Helen remarked.

'She grows more like her every day.' He glanced across at his daughter, smiling fondly.

While he talked about Jenny, the things they'd done together and the places they'd visited, Helen listened and even made

174

appropriate comments, but her mind was elsewhere.

Her mind was with the man who loved her, the man who wanted to marry her.

Her heart filled with a sudden warmth. It hadn't been much of a proposal. He had claimed to love her while looking as if he longed to shake her until her teeth rattled.

She hoped that one day they would laugh about that. She wished they could laugh about it now. She wished she could just see him . . .

'I miss her music,' Matthew was saying.

'Did she play?'

'The cello.' He smiled. 'She was very talented. And when she wasn't playing, she loved to listen. The house was always filled with music.'

Whoever fell in love with Matthew, Helen realised, would have a hard job competing against Jenny's ghost.

Suddenly, she was overwhelmed by a sense of relief. She would never fall in love with Matthew, just as he would never fall in love with her.

She had been infatuated but nothing more. Like many women, she'd been attracted to Matthew, and like them, she'd half-dreamed of being the one to take Jenny's place in his heart.

But that wasn't love. Joe had been right. Some of her feelings had stemmed from sympathy for Matthew's loss.

One day, Matthew would fall in love again, and when he did, Jenny's ghost would be finally laid to rest. She would be, once again, just an ordinary woman who had loved her husband and daughter, and who had died too young. Meanwhile, Matthew would get by, not knowing quite what he wanted. Unlike Joe, who knew exactly what he wanted, and who . . . And for the first time, Helen knew what she wanted, too.

Kerry returned to show them her collection of shells, including the special one reserved for Tom, and they went home.

Kerry fell asleep within minutes of climbing into the car, and Helen could have followed suit. But it wasn't fair to Matthew to let him drive all the way with no one to talk to, so she forced herself to stay awake.

It was late when they got home — too late to call Joe. The lights had been on in the house, but as Helen walked up the path, they went out one by one. She opened the front door, and collided with Sarah.

'Hello, Mum. You're surely not going out at this time of night?'

'Yes, I am.' Sarah looked white. 'Helen, I'm afraid I've got some bad news for you.'

Icy fingers tightened around Helen's heart. 'Not Dad?'

'No, your dad's fine. It's Melanie.'

8

Joe fumbled with his keys, finally got into the shop, rushed over to the phone and picked it up. 'First Editions?'

'Joe, it's Helen. I won't be in until late, I'm afraid.'

He could hear a tremor in her voice and hoped they hadn't had bad news. 'Problems?'

'Yes.' There was a long pause before she spoke again, very quietly and very calmly. 'Melanie was rushed into hospital last night. Mum's been there with Paul all night, but she has to go to the yard now. Apparently Paul's very shaken, and Mum thinks he needs someone with him.'

'Of course.' Joe wished he could be with her, help her, but this was a family matter and he wasn't family.

'I don't know what time I'll be in — '

'Don't worry about it.' Joe said quickly. 'I'll cope. I just hope Melanie's OK.'

'I'll let you know when there's any news. You haven't forgotten you're meeting Mr Headley for lunch?'

'Of course not. I'll close the shop for an hour or so.'

'There's no need,' Helen replied. 'I'll sort something out. I think Cassie should be able to help out. It's only a case of answering the phone and telling people we'll be back shortly.'

'It's not important for heavens' sake!'

'No, but leave it with me. I'd better go. Expect me when you see me.'

Joe replaced the receiver with a long sigh. He wished he meant as much to Helen as this shop did. She was going to shut him out again, he knew it. When she had problems, and she seemed to have more than her fair share at the moment, she would cope alone.

Perhaps he was being unfair. When her father had been so ill, there had certainly been times when she'd seemed glad to turn to him . . .

He couldn't even begin to imagine how Paul was feeling. If he had been in Paul's shoes, if Helen had been having their child . . . If, if, if!

The morning passed quickly. Joe had just made himself a coffee when he spotted Matthew Anderson on the other side of the road.

He'd been dismayed to hear that the Lyndhursts' neighbour was taking Helen out. All right, it had only been for a picnic, and Matthew's little girl had been there . . . but

179

Joe had still hoped Helen wouldn't enjoy the afternoon.

Matthew was heading for the shop now, hoping to see Helen, no doubt.

The door opened, and Joe fixed a polite smile in place, ready to take great delight in telling him that he was out of luck.

'Hello, Joe,' Matthew greeted him. 'Helen said you might need some help.'

Joe stared at him.

'She said you had a lunch appointment?' Matthew added. 'I believe I'm supposed to answer the phone and deal with the customers in your absence.'

Of all the people in the all the world, Helen has asked Matthew Anderson to help out in the shop. In *their* shop.

'Well — it's very kind of you.' Joe managed to say, but there was little gratitude behind the words.

'Cassie was first choice,' Matthew informed him with a smile, 'but she's busy at the hotel.'

'I see.'

With a supreme effort, Joe showed him where everything was and even made him a coffee.

It should have been impossible to dislike Matthew Anderson. He seemed a totally amiable chap. But Joe disliked the man intensely.

'How was your picnic?' he asked.

'Very enjoyable, thanks.' Matthew gave him a curious sideways look. 'The weather was perfect.'

'I know,' Joe said shortly.

'Kerry enjoyed herself, of course. She enjoys being with Helen.' He smiled. 'In fact, Helen's second on her list of possible stepmothers. Her teacher's first on the list, and she must be about sixty.'

Joe looked at the heavy, leather-bound book sitting on the counter. He could cheerfully have thrown it in Matthew's face. As if all the man had to do was click his fingers!

He took a deep breath.

'How about you? Who's first on your list?'

'I don't have a list.' Matthew raised his eyebrows slightly at Joe's expression. 'I have no plans for marriage at the moment.'

'At the moment.' What did that mean — when he'd grown tired of toying with Helen?

He knew he ought to feel sorry for Matthew. He'd lost his wife, after all. But all he saw was a man who could get Helen running round in circles — effortlessly.

It was too early to leave for his lunch appointment, but Joe couldn't stay in Anderson's company a minute longer.

181

Sarah nearly missed Alex Monroe at the yard.

After a night by Melanie's side, telling Paul not to worry when there was nothing else he could do, she'd come to the office, sorted out everything that had to be done, and was on her way to visit Tom, before going back to the maternity hospital.

She wasn't sure what to tell Tom about Mel. Perhaps she wouldn't tell him anything until they had further news . . .

What she really wanted to do was stand in the middle of the yard and scream. What had any of them done to deserve this?

From the look on his face, Alex wasn't the bearer of glad tidings, either.

'Did you want me?' Sarah asked. 'I was just on my way to the hospital.'

'We've got problems, I'm afraid, Sarah.'

Don't I know it, Sarah thought.

'You know Mike Simpson's off sick? We'll soon be three men short. Terry Waters has given a week's notice.'

'You said three men?'

'That's right. Jim Finch is leaving in two weeks.'

'But why?'

'He's going to Smythes.' Alex named their chief rivals. 'And Terry's setting up on his

182

own. I think the men are worried that their jobs aren't too safe without Tom keeping an eye on things.'

'Terrific. How big a problem is it, Alex?'

'Big enough,' Alex admitted. 'With the golf club contract to complete, this isn't the best of times. Even if we can replace them, it's not good having new men start in the middle of a job.'

'You said 'if' we can replace them,' Sarah pointed out. 'Surely, with all the unemployment around, there must be dozens of men after work.'

'You could be right,' Alex said. 'There is some good news though.' He pointed across the yard. 'The timber for the window frames arrived this morning.'

'The timber that should have been here two weeks ago?'

'The very same. I was beginning to worry about that.'

Sarah glanced at her watch.

'I've got to dash, Alex. Have a word with Linda, will you? Tell her to contact the Job Centre and get some ads in the local papers. Whatever else happens, we have to finish at the golf club on schedule.'

★ ★ ★

Paul sat by Melanie's bed in the small, impersonal room.

The maternity ward was next door, and Paul had seen proud fathers going to visit the happy mothers. If the circumstances had been different, Melanie would have been in the ward herself.

Born too early, small and vulnerable, their son had been rushed into the special care baby unit. They didn't know whether they'd ever be able to take him home.

The doctor had warned Paul that Melanie was very weak, but that her emotional state was giving more concern than her physical well-being. Paul had been told all this, but they hadn't told him how to deal with it.

'Your mum was here all night,' Paul told his wife, trying to keep his voice light and optimistic. 'Helen's been here all morning, but she's gone back to the shop now. She said she'd call in this evening.'

Melanie shrugged.

'I don't know why. There's nothing to see.'

'I imagine she'd like to see her sister. And her nephew,' Paul added quietly.

Melanie didn't answer for a long time.

'I'm tired, Paul,' she said at last. 'Perhaps you ought to go.'

Paul didn't know what to do.

'I'll stay.' He leaned across and kissed her.

'You try and sleep. I'll be right here.'

Melanie closed her eyes, but he didn't expect her to sleep.

Paul walked over to the window and watched the people walking into the building. They all wore identical smiles, brimming with excitement and wonder at the miracle of life, and they all carried gifts for mothers and babies.

It was so simple for them. In a few days, the mothers would take their babies home and life would go on . . .

Paul went and sat by Melanie's bed again. He knew she wasn't asleep, and he knew they couldn't keep ignoring the issue. She must need him . . . he certainly needed her.

'They can work miracles these days, Mel,' he said gently.

Melanie opened her eyes.

'I won't have more children, Paul,' she said, her voice suddenly stronger. 'I'm not going through this again. I mean it.'

'Stop it, darling,' Paul said softly. 'I married you because I love you, not because I wanted dozens of children. If we don't have any more children, we don't. But we have a son, Mel.'

Melanie turned her face away and closed her eyes.

Paul sat by her side, feeling helpless. She still refused to talk about their son. She hadn't been able to hold him, and had only seen him briefly before he was whisked away.

The doctor had told Paul to be prepared for these bouts of depression. He'd said it was her way of coping.

She believed that, if she didn't talk about their child, didn't think about him, and didn't acknowledge his existence, it wouldn't hurt so much if he didn't live.

But it would. Paul knew it would.

A doctor and two nurses arrived, and Paul was grateful to step outside for a while. He was relieved that he didn't have Sarah or Helen here at the moment, trying to drown him in sweet tea.

He hadn't thanked either of them for their company, he realised belatedly. They'd each helped in their own way.

Sarah had kept her mind on practical matters like informing his parents, making sure the house was locked, and such like.

Helen had been content to sit quietly with him, seeming to know that he didn't want to talk.

He walked along to the special care unit. There was a window on the side wall, and he stood there, gazing at the tiny form in the incubator, half-hidden by tubing. A large label above the boy's head read, 'Boy. Gibson'.

My son, Paul thought. And while his son fought for every breath, there wasn't a single thing Paul could do to help. He couldn't even hold him.

He'd wanted to give Melanie and their baby everything money could buy. Now, he would give everything he had just to be able to hold his son.

Paul felt a gentle touch on his arm and turned to look, through a blur of tears, at one of the nurses. The tears poured down his face, and he couldn't stop them.

'Can I get you something, Mr Gibson?' she asked gently. 'Tea? Coffee? Something to eat?'

Paul shook his head.

The nurse looked through the window.

'He's quite a fighter.'

Paul rubbed the tears from his face.

'His name — ' He cleared his throat and tried again. 'His name is Thomas Paul.'

'I'll let everyone know,' she promised.

'Thank you.' Paul strode back to Melanie's room.

★ ★ ★

Helen felt totally drained when she reached the shop. The morning spent with Paul had exhausted her.

Joe was talking to a customer. With a quick

smile in his direction, she went into the back room and put the kettle on. Joe didn't look very happy, she noticed.

Perhaps his meeting hadn't gone as well as they'd hoped. They were being allowed to handle the sale of the vast library that had belonged to Mr Headley's great-aunt. Today's lunch appointment with Mr Headley had been simply to sort out the arrangements, Helen hoped.

The tinkling of the doorbell signalled the departure of the customer, and Helen carried two cups of coffee into the shop.

'How did it go?'

'Fine. How's Melanie?'

'Paul was on his way to see her when I left,' Helen said. 'She's in no danger, but the baby — they had a boy — no one's too optimistic about him.'

'I'm sorry,' Joe said with a shake of his head. 'It seemed as if everything was going right for them, didn't it? Perhaps — '

'Yes,' Helen said softly. 'Perhaps there will be better news about the baby tomorrow. So how did it go with Mr Headley?' she asked, changing to an easier subject.

'It's all very straightforward,' Joe answered. 'In fact, I don't know why we had to discuss it over lunch. A phone call would have been OK.'

'You don't seem very thrilled.' Helen frowned.

'I'm thrilled,' Joe said, sounding anything but. 'There are some valuable books there — we'll have to go round and make an inventory. I suggested Sunday, but — ' He glanced at her. 'Perhaps you have other plans?'

'No,' Helen said, puzzled.

The phone rang, and Joe went to answer it.

Throughout those long hours at the hospital with Paul, the only thing that had kept her going had been the thought of coming back to Joe, but now he seemed so distant.

'What's wrong?' Helen asked when he finished his call.

'Wrong?' He glanced up.

'Something's wrong. You have a face like a wet weekend and you don't seem to give tuppence about Headley's library.'

'Put it down to a morning spent in Matthew Anderson's company.'

'A morning? How long was he here, for heaven's sake?'

'OK then, half an hour in his company. Half an hour too long!'

Helen was speechless, and then felt mounting anger.

'Joe — for heaven's sake, how petty can you get?'

Joe slammed a book shut, increasing Helen's anger.

'Well, pardon me,' she snapped. 'I was under the impression — and so was Matthew — that he was doing us a favour. Perhaps you'd rather we closed the shop in future?'

'I would!'

'My sister is in hospital,' Helen said. 'I had neither the time nor the inclination to chase around. Matthew was next door and he was the first person I thought of.'

'He always is the first person you think of. Perhaps you'd like me to sell him my half of our so-called partnership. That way you could have your cosy little picnics on Sundays, and be with him in your shop during the week!'

'Perhaps that's not such a bad idea!' Helen was shaking with temper. 'Do you know — after our cosy little picnic, I was going to phone you. Fortunately we got back too late. Then Melanie was taken into hospital . . . I was going to tell you that I wanted to marry you. Can you believe that? Whatever possessed me to think that marriage to you was worth even considering, God alone knows!'

With that, she stormed off into the back room. She had to get away from him.

She took several deep breaths, and then her

mind filled with the picture of Joe as she'd left him, his forehead creased as he very slowly went over every word she'd thrown at him. Such a boyish expression — and so very endearing.

She heard his steps approaching, slow, uncertain, and quickly turned her attention to the filing cabinet.

She was expecting him to speak, and she jumped a mile when his arms went around her waist. But she wouldn't give in that easily.

'That wasn't much of an acceptance speech,' he murmured in her ear.

Helen turned around to face him, ending very satisfactorily in the circle of his arms. 'As I recall, it wasn't much of a proposal!'

'No.' He smiled. 'Helen, will you marry me? Please?'

'Yes.'

The boyish expression was back on his face, an irresistible mixture of joy and wonder.

How long have I known him? Helen wondered. And why did it take me so long to realise?

Then Joe kissed her. She had never before felt so completely happy.

They both went through the rest of the working day walking on air.

'You don't want a long engagement, do you?' Joe asked some time that afternoon, and she laughed softly.

'No. But I would like Dad to give me away. He's getting better every day.'

'Of course,' Joe said.

'And we need somewhere to live,' Helen pointed out. 'Somewhere in the country would be nice, wouldn't it?'

'Perfect,' Joe agreed, beaming at her. 'I don't care where it is as long as you're living in it with me.'

'A bit expensive perhaps — '

'We'll give ourselves a pay rise.'

'A pay rise?' Helen asked innocently. 'I thought you were selling your half of our so-called partnership to Matthew.'

Joe laughed.

'What I am going to do is to make sure my ring is on your finger before the day's over. Just so he gets the message.

'And I'm sorry I was such a pain. I know you've had a rough day, and I'm truly sorry about Melanie. It was just the thought of you spending yesterday with him, and then turning to him this morning. Besides, he's such a smooth — '

Laughing, Helen slipped her arms around his neck. The last customer had just gone out, and she kissed him tenderly.

'I love you so much, Joe.'

Joe covered her face with kisses, pausing just long enough to promise, 'I'll do everything I can to make you happy.'

★ ★ ★

Sarah breathed a sigh of relief as the front door opened signalling the arrival of Cassie and Helen. It sounded as if Joe was with them, too.

She'd been looking forward to this day so much — Tom's first trial day at home. It had seemed like a dream come true, the first real step on the path back to normality. The reality had been very different from the dream, though.

Tom had expected to shut himself in the room he used as a study, and spend the day on the phone. Sarah had very firmly put her foot down, so he had proceeded to jump down her throat at the slightest thing.

She escaped to the kitchen the moment the girls and Joe came in, whilst the three of them chatted to Tom. They could tease him, and make him laugh. Sarah couldn't, not today. She couldn't even talk to him. During almost thirty years of marriage, there hadn't been a time when she'd felt unable to turn to Tom, to confide in him, to seek his reassurance, until now.

She went through with the tea, and Joe took the tray from her.

'It's good to see you, Joe,' Tom said. 'We don't see nearly enough of you.'

'You'll be seeing a lot more of him in future,' Helen said happily. 'And he had to come today because he wants a word with you.'

'Oh?'

'He wants to ask for your daughter's hand in marriage,' Helen said, smiling.

A stunned silence met her words, but the entire room was lit by Tom's smile. Sarah wasn't sure if it was Helen's news or that smile which brought tears springing to her eyes. It was the first genuine smile, a real Tom sort of smile, that she'd seen since he had his accident.

Then everyone started talking at once.

'It's about time we had some good news, love.' Sarah hugged Helen tight. 'And this is the best.'

Joe accepted the hugs, kisses and congratulations as if he was a man who held the sun, the moon and the stars in his hands. What he actually held was an antique ring, a ruby guarded by a circle of diamonds.

'We chose this last week,' he explained, 'but Helen refused to wear it until we'd made the

194

announcement. And we thought today, with Tom being here, was the only day we could choose.'

'You daft pair,' Tom grinned, too touched to say more.

As Joe slipped the ring on Helen's finger and kissed her, Sarah felt a sudden surge of pride. Like herself, when their eldest daughter gave her heart, she gave it completely. And she couldn't have given it to a better man.

There would be no worries where Helen and Joe were concerned. No matter what the future held in store for them both, they would face it together.

Sarah only wished the same could be said about Melanie and Paul.

'This calls for something a little better than tea,' Tom announced. 'What have we got, Sarah?'

'Whatever it is, we've got something better,' Helen said happily. 'Champagne that's probably getting very warm in the car.'

Helen and Joe went to get it together, and Sarah smiled to herself. They wanted to do everything together, but they also wanted a few moments alone.

'I'll get some glasses,' Cassie said.

Cassie had made all the right noises, but Sarah knew her heart wasn't in it. Since the day Ian had put his ring on her finger, she had watched Melanie marry Paul, and soon she would watch Helen walk down the aisle.

Sarah sat in the chair next to Tom's.

'Joe looks like a ten-year-old with a new bike,' she said.

'I know just how he feels.' Tom reached for Sarah's held and squeezed it tight. 'I know I've been a bit touchy lately but — '

'That must be the understatement of the decade,' Sarah teased.

'It all takes so long,' Tom complained. 'The way we're going, I shall still be stuck in that hospital this time next year!'

'Rubbish,' Sarah scoffed. 'The doctors are amazed at how well you're doing.'

'I want to get back to normal,' Tom insisted. 'I want to get back to work, to get out in the garden. And most of all I want to see my grandson.'

'Yes, well,' Sarah murmured. 'There's plenty of time for that.'

As far as Tom was aware, his namesake was premature but doing nicely. She hadn't wanted to worry him with details.

The champagne was opened with a flourish.

'Have you decided on a date yet?' Tom asked.

'No,' Joe replied. 'It's as soon as you can

196

walk down the aisle and hand her over to me!'

'Book the church,' Tom declared. 'I'll soon be out of that place.'

Sarah shook her head in amusement. But at least this wedding would give Tom something to look forward to, other than getting back to work.

For the first time she felt cautiously optimistic. Tom was on the road to recovery, slow though it might be. Helen and Joe had just given them wonderful news. And as for Thomas Paul Junior, perhaps he would pull through.

In the midst of the celebrations, Matthew and Kerry called in.

Sarah was curious, noticing the unmistakable tension between Joe and Matthew. But if it was difficult to judge Matthew's feelings, Kerry's views were made very plain.

'I wanted you to marry Daddy,' she told Helen, and her bottom lip quivered.

Helen moved to put her arm around Kerry, but the child pulled away.

'I've already promised to marry Joe,' Helen said lightly. 'I can't marry your daddy as well, can I?'

'I don't like Joe,' Kerry muttered mutinously.

'Kerry!' Matthew scolded sharply.

'That's a pity,' Helen said innocently. 'We were hoping you'd be one of my bridesmaids. Never mind, I'll have to ask someone else.'

Kerry looked up at Helen, then at Joe, then back at Helen.

'Are you having a proper dress? A long white one?'

'Of course,' Helen assured her. 'But if you're not interested . . . '

'Would I have a long dress?' Kerry asked.

'I think so. I was hoping Cassie would help me choose the dresses. She's much better at that sort of thing than I am.'

'Would I have to carry flowers?' Kerry persisted. 'And be on all the photos?'

Tom couldn't suppress a chuckle.

'That's what we'd hoped for,' Joe said. 'But as you're not interested, we'll ask someone else. In fact, I think I know the very person . . . '

'All right,' Kerry accepted ungraciously. 'I'll do it.' She looked at Joe for a long time. 'I suppose you're quite nice really.'

'I suppose I am,' Joe agreed gravely, and Sarah saw that wide smile back on Tom's face.

Soon afterwards, Helen noticed that Cassie had slipped away. She found her sister in the garden, sitting on the old wooden seat, staring into space.

Helen sat beside her. 'All this wedding talk must be making you feel awful.'

'No.' Cassie smiled. 'I'm happy for you. Really. Joe's smashing.'

Helen could see right through that smile to the unhappiness beneath.

'Will you help me choose the dresses and suchlike? And I'm taking it for granted that you'll be bridesmaid. You will, won't you?'

'Try stopping me.' Cassie grinned with some of her old sparkle. 'And don't think I've come out here because I can't bear to hear the word wedding mentioned,' she added seriously. 'I was just thinking about Mel. And that poor baby. So tiny and so — unloved.'

'He's not unloved,' Helen said. 'Melanie's just too scared to love him in case — well, in case he doesn't make it. And Paul's hardly gone home all week. When he's not with Melanie, he's looking through that awful glass window and willing little Thomas to live. If that baby lives, he'll be spoilt rotten. He'll be the biggest miracle ever.'

'If he lives,' Cassie said quietly.

'Joe asked me to marry him before he was born,' she confided, 'and I'd already decided to say yes. But if I hadn't, the sight of little Thomas would have made up my mind. Every time I see him, I know that the only children I could have are Joe's. And I know

199

that if I were in Melanie's shoes, the only person who could get me through it would be Joe.'

Cassie sprang to her feet, mumbled something that Helen didn't catch and ran back to the house, almost colliding with Joe as she went.

'Was it something I said?' he asked Helen.

'No.' Helen sighed. 'It was something I said. Poor Cassie.'

'I just came to say I think your mum wants to get rid of us,' Joe told her.

He was right. Sarah was delighted that they'd been able to celebrate Tom's brief escape from hospital in such style, but she was relieved when Cassie left with Matthew and Kerry and Joe and Helen went soon afterwards.

She didn't want Tom returning to the hospital worn out, or they might not let him back home for a while.

Once they were alone, they manoeuvred Tom's wheelchair into the garden and sat quietly together. At least, Sarah sat quietly, enjoying the peace and quiet, while Tom listed all the jobs that needed doing in the garden.

When the doorbell rang, Sarah thought it would be the ambulance to take Tom back.

She was surprised to see a policeman on

the doorstep. The surprise was quickly followed by a cold feeling of dread.

'Is Mr Lyndhurst in?' he asked.

'Yes — well, what exactly is the problem? I'm Mrs Lyndhurst.'

'I'd really like to see Mr Lyndhurst.'

'You can't,' Sarah said, her breath coming in short gasps. 'He's under strict medical supervision. What is it?'

'I'm afraid there's been a fire at his premises in Castle Road.'

9

Sarah stood in the middle of Lyndhurst's yard, unable to utter a single word. Alex Monroe was with her, and so was Linda, but no one spoke.

Policemen were striding about, talking to each other or into their radios. A reporter was trying to talk to them whilst his colleague took photographs by the roll. But mostly, people just stood and stared.

Sarah hadn't imagined a fire on this scale. She wanted to say something to shake Alex and Linda out of their numbed shock. She wanted to tell them that they must look on the bright side, and that things could have been worse. Tears welled up, a mixture of anger and despair, and she quickly blinked them back.

What would Tom do in the circumstances? He certainly wouldn't burst into tears. He would swear a lot, shout a lot more, and then he would get down to business.

And that's what Sarah must do.

She was glad Tom was safely back in hospital, glad he was still unaware of the fire. The ambulance had arrived seconds after the policeman and Sarah had asked the policeman to move his panda car before Tom was wheeled out.

She'd never know how she'd stayed so icy calm, laughing and joking as she'd helped her husband into the ambulance. It had been hard to linger at the hospital, having seen him into bed, but she knew he mustn't be suspicious.

They'd come so far with his recovery, Sarah was determined that there would be no more setbacks. And Dr Patrick, whom she'd seen briefly on her way out, entirely agreed.

So Sarah, and Tom's assistant, and his secretary had to handle this disaster alone.

'How did it start?' Linda said blankly. 'That's what I can't understand.'

'No one knows,' Alex said. 'I expect they'll find out eventually. Meanwhile — ' his voice trailed away.

'At least the offices are still standing,' Sarah said. 'Let's go inside. I feel like a circus exhibit standing here.'

The offices, built near the road, had a reassuring look of normality.

'Let's put the kettle on,' Sarah said, managing a shaky smile. 'The nation's cure for every disaster.'

'The power's off,' Alex told her. 'The phone's out of action, too.'

'I see.' But Sarah couldn't take any of it in.

Two more policemen arrived. The older one introduced himself as Inspector Stevens. He sounded very sympathetic, but then he said, 'We'll need the names and addresses of all your employees.'

'Why?' Sarah frowned.

'Just a formality, Mrs Lyndhurst. And we'll need statements from each of you.'

'Statements?' Sarah echoed. 'What on earth for?'

'It's routine.'

It didn't feel like 'routine' as Sarah answered their many questions. In fact, she felt like a criminal.

Apparently a young boy had spotted the fire, but in the short time it took the fire brigade to arrive, the blaze was already out of control.

'We need to speak to your husband,' Inspector Stevens reminded Sarah.

'Tomorrow,' she replied firmly. 'I've spoken to his doctor. I'll talk to Tom in the morning and tell him what's happened, then you can speak to him. But we can't have him upset.'

'We quite understand,' he assured her.

When the two men left, Sarah breathed a sigh of relief. Their endless questions had lent the events of the night a sinister quality.

'That's that then,' Alex said flatly.

'Yes,' Sarah agreed. 'Perhaps we can start getting back to normal now.'

Alex and Linda exchanged a glance.

'That wasn't quite what I meant, Sarah,' Alex said. 'I admire what you've tried to do, what you're still trying to do, but you have to face facts. We're finished.'

'Finished? Oh no!'

'Look out of the window,' Alex insisted. 'You'll see thousands of pounds worth of damage.'

Sarah stared at him.

'It's all insured.'

'Of course,' Alex agreed, 'and no doubt they'll have to pay up. Eventually. But we've been struggling for months, Sarah, you know we have. The money hasn't been coming in. There's no way we can afford to replace that lot.'

'Then I'll have to see the bank manager.' Sarah knew what Alex was thinking. What bank would lend money to a firm that everyone believed to be finished? 'We'll manage.' she insisted.

'We won't,' Alex was equally firm. 'It'll be impossible to finish at the golf club on schedule now. We've got men leaving right, left and centre. The timber for those window frames held us up by — '

'We'll get more timber,' Sarah argued.

'We'll use other suppliers if necessary.'

Alex remained silent but his expression said it all. *You're the boss and you're wrong.*

Sarah felt her temper rising.

'Tomorrow, you'll be out at the golf course as if nothing has happened. I gave Compton my word that the job would be finished, and it will be. Come hell or high water!'

★ ★ ★

Cassie was chatting to the young woman from Room 107, but she was watching Nigel Emmerson as he walked the length of the reception.

The Emmerson family owned several hotels, a small chain, you might say, but until Nigel's recent arrival, the name hadn't meant very much.

Nigel, however, had big plans for expansion. He also had a knack of making the staff feel decidedly uncomfortable. His eye for detail was already legendary.

As the guest left her key and departed, Cassie checked that everything was in order on the desk.

'Good morning, Cassie.'

Nigel Emmerson spoke as if he'd only just noticed her, but Cassie knew he'd heard every word of her chat with Mary Young.

'Another lovely day, Mr Emmerson.'

'Yes.' There was a long, agonising pause before he spoke again. 'Are you happy in your work?' he asked abruptly.

'I — yes. Of course. Very happy.'

He didn't comment on that. Instead, he began walking away, and spoke over his shoulder. 'See me in my office in twenty minutes, will you?'

The doors closed after him.

Cassie stared after him, wide-eyed. 'Yes, sir!'

He's going to fire me was her first thought. She couldn't think of anything she'd done wrong but, like God, he moved in very mysterious ways.

When he'd first arrived, nice Jeannie McInnes from the restaurant was longing to mother him. By the end of his first week on the premises, Jeannie had been threatening to leave.

Cassie tried to tell herself that it didn't matter if he did fire her. There was more to life than work. She'd discovered that much since Ian had left for London.

She'd told Nigel she was happy in her work, and she was, but without Ian nothing was quite the same. In fact, she had half made up her mind to follow him to London . . .

Nowadays, she and Ian were talking on the telephone almost every day. Really talking. They were laughing together again, too. So if she was fired, it wouldn't matter at all.

Except for her pride. Above everything else, she was good at her job. No one, not even Nigel Emmerson, could tell her otherwise.

On this defiant thought, Cassie knocked on the door and strode into his office.

He was all charm, seating her opposite him and offering her coffee, which she declined.

'So, Cassie.' He leaned back in his chair. 'Tell me. What do you think of me?'

Cassie felt her eyebrows disappear into her fringe. She thought she must have misheard. Either that or it was a joke.

'You must have formed an opinion,' he prompted. 'We've been working on the same team for a month now.'

She had. But she wasn't that brave.

'Well,' she began, choosing her words with care, 'I think you're very proud of the hotel and you intend to make sure it keeps its reputation. You work hard. You expect nothing less than perfection — from yourself and from others.'

(She remembered a tearful Jeannie complaining, 'You don't know where you are with him from one minute to the next.')

'And I think you can be a little tactless at

times,' she added with her usual frankness.

Much to her surprise, he laughed at that.

'Very tactfully put. And you're right, of course. If I'd used more tact with Mrs McInnes, I wouldn't have had to spend hours persuading her to stay on.'

He shuffled through some papers on his desk, and handed a photocopy to Cassie.

'Tell me what do you think about that?'

As Cassie read it, her eyes widened. It was an ad for a new hotel post — conference facilities manager. The new facilities had been no more than rumours, but obviously the rumours were soon to be realised.

'What do you think?' he asked again.

What was she supposed to think?

'I think it's very well worded,' she said drily. 'I think the salary's a dream, and I think you'll be inundated with applicants.'

'And you think you could do the job with your eyes closed?' he suggested.

Was she very transparent, or was he more perceptive than he looked?

'I don't have the qualifications.'

'Now that's where I think you're wrong. You're very good with people. I've watched you at work and you're a genius at smoothing ruffled feathers. You're unflappable and conscientious — tactful, too,' he added ruefully.

Cassie's heart started to race. Surely he wasn't seriously suggesting . . . ?

'It's a long-term project,' he was saying. 'It's not even built yet. But we'll be offering everything the businessman needs, from the latest technology and the staff to operate it all, to all the leisure facilities imaginable.'

His eyes were shining as he took a large file from his desk.

'Let me show you the plans.'

Plans were soon spread across his desk. Cassie saw nothing more than confusing lines and squiggles, but Nigel was talking as if the businessmen were already in residence.

'Where do I come into all this?' she asked. 'You're surely not suggesting that I apply for this job?'

'I'm suggesting we try it out for three months. When it takes off, the hours will be anything but nine to five. It'll be hectic, but I think you'll find the work rewarding. After three months, we can review the situation. If either of us isn't happy, we can forget the whole thing.'

Cassie was exhilarated. Half an hour ago, she'd mentally packed her bags and gone to join Ian in London. Now she was as excited as Nigel Emmerson — the challenge appealed to her.

'Some people find me difficult to work

with,' Nigel Emmerson warned her.

He looked so puzzled by the idea that Cassie almost giggled.

'You'd have to share this office for a while,' he went on. 'In the beginning, instead of working with the guests, you'll be working with contractors, interior designers — ' He sensed her hesitation. 'You'll want to think about it, of course.'

Cassie nodded. It sounded like a dream come true, but if she took the job, she would have to see it through to the end.

And in that case, what about Ian?

'When would you like my decision?' she asked.

'Monday?'

'Fine. I'll let you know then.'

★   ★   ★

Sarah walked the long way, through the gardens, into the hospital. For once, she was in no rush to see Tom. The lawns had been cut, and the borders were a mass of colour, but Sarah had no time to appreciate them.

She was walking along the corridor when she saw Dr Patrick coming out of Tom's room. He didn't speak until they were outside the day room, safely out of earshot.

'I've had to give him something to quieten

him down, Sarah. He asked for a paper, and the nurse gave him this morning's. The fire's all over the front page.'

'Oh no!' Sarah groaned. 'That's my fault. I should have told him last night. Has he taken it very badly?'

'He has.'

'He's all right though, isn't he?'

'Yes, but none of this will do him any good, Sarah. He needs complete rest.'

'I know.' But Tom wasn't the type to rest. 'Have you seen the paper?'

'I've seen enough, and you can forget trying to dismiss it as a small fire. The photograph takes up half of the front page.'

'Oh, Lord.' Sarah took a deep breath. 'I'd better go and talk to him.'

'You'll find him a bit woozy. Try to keep him calm, Sarah.'

Even before Sarah went into his room, she knew that would be easier said than done. He was sitting in his chair by the window, with the newspaper neatly folded on his knee. Sarah's smile was met with a scowl, but then, that wasn't unusual.

'Hello, love.' Sarah went over and kissed him. 'You've seen the paper, then?'

'You know damn well I have! I'm not a complete imbecile, you know. I heard you walking along the corridor, so even I can add two and two together and put the delay down to a confab with his nibs. What story have you concocted for me today?'

'Really, Tom! You're getting paranoid. Why should we concoct stories for you?'

'I want to know what happened, Sarah. I want every detail!'

'You've seen the paper,' Sarah told him calmly, 'so you probably know more than I do.'

'Just look at it!' He practically threw the newspaper at her.

Trying to look dispassionately at the photograph of what used to be Tom's pride and joy, Sarah pulled up a chair and sat beside him. Doctor Patrick could say what he liked but this wasn't Sarah's idea of 'woozy'. She read the brief report about the 'ailing' firm and its most recent 'disaster', then handed it back to Tom.

'It doesn't say much, does it?'

'It says enough!'

'They have to sell their newspaper. If they didn't make a big thing of it, it wouldn't make much of a story, would it?'

'How the devil did the fire start?' Tom demanded. 'I've always insisted that everyone abides by the rules. You have to be so careful with timber.'

'No one knows how it started,' Sarah said

patiently. 'The Fire Brigade are still investigating. But it could have been a lot worse. No one was hurt and that's all that matters. By the way, the police will be calling on you later.'

'I bet they will,' Tom said grimly. 'It's lucky I've got a good alibi.'

'You really are getting paranoid.' Sarah laughed.

Tom glared at her.

'Stop calling me paranoid! Someone round here has to be realistic, Sarah. There are going to be lots of people ready to believe I'd put a match to the yard just to put one over on the insurance company.' He gave her a sharp glance. 'I assume the insurance cover's up to date?'

'Of course it is! Honestly, Tom, you're making far too much out of this. No one was hurt and there's absolutely nothing at all to worry about.'

'Nothing to worry about? You're a fine one to talk. Every day I see you, and every day you look more worn down with worry.'

'You certainly know how to make a woman feel good!'

Tom growled his frustration.

'If I thought I could make it to the door, I'd discharge myself!'

'Now that I *would* like to see.'

Tom let out his breath on a long sigh. There wasn't a thing he could do.

When the police came, he'd badger them for details, and the nurse who'd brought him the paper had given him some small change. When Sarah left, he'd make his way to the telephone he passed every day on his way to physiotherapy. He'd see what Alex Monroe had to say about this.

He deliberately switched to a more cheerful subject. 'How's my grandson coming along?'

The question clearly caught her unawares, and he saw the dart of pain that flashed across her face.

'Sarah?'

'He's not doing too well,' Sarah admitted. 'He's so small . . . '

Tom took her hand in his. Deep down, he'd known something must be wrong. Everyone should have been talking non-stop about the new addition to the family but, in his presence at least, they'd been strangely reticent.

'It's early days yet, love,' he said gently. 'And they can work wonders.'

'Of course they can.' Sarah nodded.

'Never write off a Lyndhurst,' he added with a smile. 'We're a lot tougher than we look.'

'He's a Gibson, not a Lyndhurst.'

'He's half Lyndhurst. That's enough.'

★ ★ ★

Paul hadn't been at his video shop since Melanie had gone into hospital. He walked in, vaguely surprised to see Susan laughing with a customer, and a family of four happily arguing over which film to hire.

There was a pile of letters on his desk, and several messages, but there was nothing of any importance.

He sat at his desk and forced himself to open the mail. The first envelope contained a reminder for an outstanding invoice. Paul was still staring blankly at it when Susan knocked on the door and came in.

'It's good to see you, Paul,' she said. 'How's Melanie?'

'She's OK,' Paul replied automatically. 'She's hoping to come home tomorrow or the day after.'

'Really? That's marvellous. She's bound to feel a lot better at home. People do, don't they?'

'I suppose so,' Paul agreed.

'And the baby?'

'We don't know when he'll be coming home,' Paul said briskly. 'So how's business?'

216

'We've been really busy the last couple of days,' she told him. 'Everyone's gone keep-fit mad. The music videos are going well, too. In fact, I thought we could have a change round. If the music section was nearer the window — '

'Good idea.' Paul couldn't even begin to care about the music videos. 'I'll leave it with you, Susan.'

'I'll have a look on Monday morning,' she promised. 'We're usually quiet then.'

'Fine.'

Seeing that he wanted to get on with some work, she turned to go, and paused at the door. 'I hope everything turns out well for you, Paul.'

Paul was moved by the quietly spoken words. He certainly hadn't done anything to deserve her concern. He must be the worst person to work for imaginable.

'Thanks,' he replied. 'And thanks for all the extra work you're doing. When things are more settled — Well, I do appreciate what you're doing and I won't forget.'

'Don't worry about it. These days you have to be grateful to have a job, don't you? And I really enjoy mine.'

When she'd gone, Paul made a mental note to make sure she had some extra days off. A pay rise, too, once life was more settled.

Perhaps Susan was right, and Melanie would feel better when she came home. She might even show some interest in their son, which was more than she was doing at the moment. She hadn't even seen him yet . . .

Paul turned his attention back to the mail. He had almost finished when Susan brought his friend Neil Hutchinson into his office.

'I spotted your car at the back,' Neil explained, 'and thought I'd call in for a coffee.' He nodded towards the shop. 'She — Susan, is it? — is making one.

'So how are you, Paul? And how's Melanie?'

'She should be home tomorrow or the day after,' Paul told him.

'That's great.'

'How are Fran and the children?'

'Fine,' Neil said, clearly relieved to be discussing easier things. 'We're off to Corfu next week, so Fran's busy packing.'

'It's all right for some!'

Susan brought them coffee and when she'd gone, Neil talked about their plans for Corfu.

All Paul could think about was the day Neil's son, Andrew, had been born. He could remember the hearty slaps on the back, wetting the baby's head, and listening to Neil talk as if no one had ever produced a child before.

218

He and Neil were supposedly the best of friends, but Neil couldn't even talk about Thomas.

Paul was relieved when they'd finished their coffee.

'I'm going to head home,' Paul said. 'Don't forget to send us a postcard.'

'Have you and Melanie booked — ?' Neil grimaced. 'No, I don't suppose you have.' There was an awkward pause. 'I'm sure he'll be all right, Paul. Some babies are having heart surgery and all manner of things done when they're only a few days old. They can do marvels these days.'

'So people keep telling me.'

'I wish there was something I could say,' Neil said awkwardly. 'I'm sorry, Paul. Fran's been wondering if Melanie's allowed visitors. She's got a couple of presents for the baby but she doesn't know whether — '

Paul's resentment vanished. Of course it was difficult. Neil and Fran would like nothing more than to shower them with congratulations and cuddly toys for Thomas.

'It would be best to leave it for a while,' he said. 'Melanie's not too bright at the moment. She hasn't even seen Thomas yet.'

'Not at all?' Neil asked incredulously.

'She won't talk about him, and she won't see him.'

'I wish there was something I could say,' Neil said again.

'I know. Thanks for coming in, Neil . . . '

When Neil left, Paul tidied up his desk and drove home.

He'd intended to check the mail and go straight back to the hospital. When he spotted Helen walking down their path he groaned aloud.

Helen was the last person he wanted to see. No, that wasn't true. It wasn't Helen. He didn't want to see anyone. All he wanted was to be left alone.

When she saw him, she walked back to her own car and took some bags from the back seat.

'Hello, Paul,' she greeted him, 'I'm glad I caught you. I've just seen Melanie, and she's given me strict instructions to cook you a meal. Sorry, but orders are orders. I've given her my word I'll cook you something. She said you had a dizzy turn at the hospital.'

'Good grief, I stood up too quickly, that's all.' Paul spoke more calmly. 'It's good of you to offer, Helen, really it is, but I don't feel like eating at the moment.'

'I know, but I promised Melanie. So either I cook you something here or you could come home and eat with us!' She smiled at his expression. 'Yes, I thought you'd rather eat here.'

He'd rather not eat anywhere.

'I bought steak,' she told him. 'It won't take long.'

Paul had little choice but to give in gracefully.

'How did Melanie seem?' he asked as Helen chopped onions in the kitchen.

'Very quiet. And she's worried about you. You don't look too good, Paul, you know. Anyone can see you haven't slept for days.'

Paul ignored that. 'Did she mention Thomas?'

'No,' Helen replied softly. 'But she'll come round. When she's home, she'll feel better. You'll see.'

'I hope so.'

Paul went to change. When he came back to the kitchen, the steaks were sizzling under the grill. Until now he hadn't stopped to think about it, but he hadn't eaten all day and he was suddenly ravenous.

'I appreciate this, Helen. And I am hungry. Starving, in fact.'

'Good. I know it's hard, Paul, but you must look after yourself. Even if you can't sleep, you should at least try to eat three times a day.'

'Yes, Miss.'

'Sorry. Joe's going to marry a terrible nag, isn't he?' Helen laughed. 'But you must try, Paul. Melanie doesn't need to be worrying about you, too.'

'I know,' Paul agreed. 'And I will try.'

As soon as they'd eaten, Helen could see that Paul was keen to get to the hospital.

'You go,' she said. 'I'll clear this lot away and lock up.'

'Are you sure?'

'Of course,' Helen smiled. 'And don't forget to tell Melanie that you've eaten! My life won't be worth living if she thinks you're fainting away from hunger.'

'I won't forget. And thanks, Helen.'

When Paul had gone, Helen washed up and tidied the kitchen. She had no idea what he'd eat tomorrow. The fridge had six pints of milk in it, but there was nothing in the cupboards. She decided to do some shopping in the morning.

Paul's diet was the least of her worries, though. What worried Helen most was that Melanie and Paul didn't seem able to share their problems. Each had told Helen enough to know they worried about the other, but it didn't seem right. They should be confiding in each other, not in her.

If she were in Melanie's shoes, Helen knew she wouldn't want Joe out of her sight for a moment. Even if she felt she had to shut out the rest of the world, she would need Joe.

She'd have to get her skates on. She and Joe were going to look at a couple of possible places that evening and if she didn't get a move on, Joe would go without her.

She suspected he'd be only too happy to view the old vicarage alone and then tell her it was unsuitable. Helen had fallen in love with the place from the photograph, but Joe, infuriatingly practical, had spent an hour pointing out the disadvantages.

The telephone rang — probably Joe. Helen ran to answer it.

'Is Mr Gibson there?' a male voice asked.

'He isn't, I'm afraid. I'm his sister-in-law. Can I take a message?'

'My name's Gordon Turner. I wonder if you'd know where I could get hold of him.'

Helen recognised the name — it was the paediatric consultant. Thomas's doctor.

'He's on his way to the hospital, Mr Turner. He should be with you any minute.'

She hung up, a cold fear suddenly gripping her. For baby Thomas, for her sister, and for Paul . . .

10

As soon as word spread that little Thomas had lost his brave battle for life, the whole community had rallied round to offer what support they could.

Sarah, stopping her car outside Melanie's and waving to the neighbour who was just leaving, wondered if these people knew how much their kindness helped. Whether it was flowers from their garden, a chat over a cup of tea, or just a sympathetic voice on the end of a phone, it had helped enormously during the last six weeks.

Not that Sarah could stop worrying about Melanie. She'd called in often, unable to believe that Melanie was coping as well as she claimed to be, and convinced she needed her mother to lean on.

'I am popular today,' Melanie said, giving Sarah a quick hug. 'You're my fourth visitor.'

As they went into the sitting-room, Sarah wondered if so many well-wishers might be getting Melanie down. 'They mean well, love.'

'Oh, I know,' Melanie said quickly. 'I wasn't complaining.' She smiled. 'I never knew we had so many friends.'

'How are you coping, Melanie? Really?' Sarah sat down.

'I'm OK.'

'I'm your mother, Melanie.' Sarah wasn't convinced. 'You don't have to put on a brave face for me. You can have a good cry if you like.'

'I have cried,' Melanie replied quietly. 'For the first couple of weeks, I couldn't, but since then I've cried all right. There are no tears left now.

'But I'm OK, Mum,' she went on. 'The other day, I went into the church. I was feeling sorry for myself, thinking that Thomas should have been christened there. I just sat there on my own. I didn't pray or anything. I was looking at that stained glass window. The tall one.'

Sarah swallowed hard. 'The one of the shepherd and the lambs?'

'Yes. And while I was sitting there, I suddenly felt — I don't know really — that there was something there, all around me. I felt at peace, and calm. And safe.' She smiled a little ruefully. 'That sounds ridiculous, doesn't it.'

'It doesn't, Melanie,' Sarah said brokenly. 'No, it doesn't.'

Longing to comfort Melanie, she was

unable to do or say anything. The tears poured down her face, and it was Melanie who turned to take Sarah in her arms.

'It's all right, Mum,' Melanie said gently. 'Really it is. That's what I'm trying to tell you. Whatever happened while I was sitting in the church made me see things more clearly. I knew then that we'd have other babies, and that they would be all right.'

'That's supposed to be my line,' Sarah said with a weak smile, brushing her tears away. 'I come here to cheer you up, and just look at me!'

'Dry your eyes,' Melanie said softly, 'and I'll put the kettle on.'

When Melanie returned with the tray, her mother had dried her face and put a comb through her hair. Along with tea and biscuits, Melanie had brought a selection of holiday brochures.

'What on earth are those for?' Sarah asked in amazement.

Melanie laughed.

'Usually they're for holidays! Paul doesn't know it yet but we're going on a holiday. I have to drag him out of that shop, and out of his depression. His heart's not in anything at the moment.'

'It's bound to take time, love.'

'I know but normally he's — well, you

know what he's like, Mum. Full of enthusiasm, and jumping from one harebrained scheme to the next. At least, you'd call them harebrained.'

'That's not — '

'Mum,' Melanie interrupted with a fond smile, 'I know Paul annoys you and Dad sometimes.'

'Not really.' Sarah crossed her fingers. 'We like him,' she added lamely.

'And I love him,' Melanie replied with conviction. 'Right now, nothing would make me happier than to see Paul as he used to be — as he should be — full of enthusiasm and bursting with wild ideas. That's the way he is, Mum, and that's the way I want him.'

Sarah was left gasping by this new, decisive Melanie. Clearly she was coping — and very well, at that.

'So I'm taking him away.' Melanie opened one of the brochures. 'It won't solve all our problems, I know, but it will be a step in the right direction.' She turned the pages. 'Portugal looks nice. What do you think?'

They browsed for the next hour, and when Sarah had to leave, Melanie seemed settled on Portugal.

'I think it's a marvellous idea.' Sarah paused at the door. 'I'm proud of you, Melanie. I really am. You're a lesson to us all.'

She hugged her tight. 'Where did all this strength and wisdom come from?'

'I don't know,' Melanie admitted. 'Perhaps it was that day in the church. Perhaps there's a part of you in me after all — and a part of Dad. I honestly don't know, Mum. I just know Paul needs me to be strong just now.'

When her husband came home that evening, Melanie showed him the brochures. Once his initial surprise had worn off, he gave her a dozen reasons why they shouldn't go away.

'It's a bad time, Mel. The shop's busy and I can't keep leaving everything to Susan. If we left it until the spring — '

'The shop will be just as busy.' Melanie knew he was inventing excuses. 'And Susan knows what she's doing.'

They discussed it until Paul finally lost interest. He really couldn't care one way or the other, Melanie realised, and she went to bed even more determined to ring the travel agent's first thing in the morning.

She wasn't sure what woke her, but the clock display told her it was just after four.

Paul was standing by the window. She switched on the lamp, got out of bed and went to his side. He didn't speak — or couldn't speak. Tears were rolling down his cheeks.

'Paul, don't.'

She offered her hand and he clasped it tight.

'I wanted to give you so much,' he said at last. 'You and Thomas. I wanted to give you everything. And now — ' Tears choked him.

'I still need you, Paul,' Melanie said urgently. 'We'll have other children and they'll need you, too.' Very gently, she brushed his tears away. 'We're young, we've got a good marriage. We've got the rest of our lives in front of us. We have to look to the future.'

Paul turned and took her into his arms.

'You're right, I know you are.' He kissed the top of her head. 'I'm sorry. It's just that sometimes — '

'I know,' Melanie whispered.

'You're cold,' Paul said. 'Let's go back to bed.'

Lying with Paul's arms around her, Melanie thought again of Portugal.

'We'll have a good holiday, Paul. It will do us good to get away from everything.'

'You're right,' Paul agreed sleepily. 'Perhaps we'll fall in love with the place and decide to stay. We could open a restaurant.'

'What!' Melanie's eyes widened with horror at the thought. Then, slowly, the horror changed to amusement. She fell asleep with a smile on her lips.

'I can't believe all this is ours,' Helen said happily.

'Believe it.' Joe laughed. 'Every creaking door, every rotten window frame, and every inch of flaking paint — it's all ours.'

Laughing, Helen caught his hand. They walked across what had once been a lawn to the bottom of the garden, and sat on a pile of stones.

'Was this once a wall?' Helen asked and Joe wrapped his arms around her.

'Who knows? We'll need a garden seat if we're going to sit here and admire the missing roof tiles.'

Helen had to admit that the house showed signs of neglect, but it seemed such a happy place. Inside, it was a wonder of nooks and crannies, and small windows with wide sills, all waiting to hold treasured possessions. It was a house of character. What stories the house could tell, she thought. And the best story of all was only just beginning.

'I can't wait to start on the garden, Joe.'

'I can't wait to move in!'

'You can move in any time,' Helen pointed out. 'It's silly to keep on your flat.'

'That wasn't exactly what I had in mind.'

He laughed. 'A November wedding would be nice.'

'I was thinking more of Easter,' Helen replied quietly.

'But that's months away!' He lifted her chin. 'You're not having second thoughts, are you?'

He looked so concerned that Helen shrieked with laughter and threw her arms around his neck.

'Darling Joe, of course I'm not. But there's a lot to arrange, and I want everything to be perfect. When we're celebrating our golden wedding anniversary, I want to be able to look at the photos and remember the happiest day of our lives.'

'All the planning in the world won't make it any more memorable.'

'Humour me,' Helen pleaded, and Joe shook his head with amusement.

'Do I ever do anything else? Easter it is, then. And perhaps you're right. It will probably take us till then to get this place habitable, don't you think?'

'Let's go back inside and decide what we'll start on first.'

They went from room to room, making plans for the future.

'We had a postcard from Melanie and Paul this morning,' Helen remarked.

'How are they enjoying Portugal?'

'Very much. The weather's been good, and Paul's very tanned. They'll be home the day after tomorrow, so we'll hear all about it then.'

'You'll have to get Melanie talking weddings,' Joe replied. 'That might cheer her up.'

'Yes, although I think Melanie's coping better than Paul,' Helen said thoughtfully. 'Just when we expected Melanie to really go to pieces, she's surprised us all.'

'But what a terrible way to learn.'

Helen nodded, and turned her face to the window to hide the tears that occasionally threatened without warning.

Joe placed a gentle hand on her shoulder.

'I wish I could promise you a life filled with nothing but happiness, Helen, but I can't. We'll have our own share of problems. But I do promise you this — whatever happens, we'll get through it together. I'll always be here for you, always.'

Helen gazed at him through a blur of tears. 'I know. That's what makes it so perfect . . . '

'Come on.' Joe reached for her hand. 'Let's go.'

'Where?'

'The garden centre. We'll buy our new

home a present — something that will grow with us.'

Helen laughed, a shaky sound that failed to convey her complete happiness.

'You romantic fool!'

★   ★   ★

Sarah had thought she would never see this day. She was actually standing in the bar at the golf club, with a glass of champagne in her hand, celebrating the completion of Lyndhurst's renovation. And the best part of all was having Tom at her side.

This get-together was a kind gesture from the committee of the golf club. Perhaps they were as relieved, and surprised, as Sarah was that the work had been finished on time. They knew about Tom's illness, of course, and the fire, but they had no idea of the million and one other things that had gone wrong. They would never know of the hours Sarah had spent on the telephone, bluffing it out with suppliers, chasing orders, hassling the insurance company.

But she'd done it. Today she felt justified in celebrating, because the business was well and truly back on its feet. And Sarah had put it there.

Gerald Compton made his way over to them.

'Congratulations, Sarah.' He put out his hand.

'Thank you.'

'I must admit,' he confided, 'I had my doubts that you could pull this one off.'

You weren't alone, Sarah thought drily, but she smiled sweetly at him.

'You must be very proud, Tom,' Compton said.

'Yes,' Tom murmured. 'Very proud.'

'I hope you won't slip back into retirement, Sarah.'

'There's no fear of that,' she assured him quickly. 'From now on it will be a real partnership which means — ' Her voice faltered as Tom crossed the room to talk to someone else. 'Which means we'll be twice as efficient.'

While Sarah accepted the congratulations that came her way, she was watching Tom, who kept on the other side of the room for the rest of the reception.

Before they'd left home, he'd made his views clear on 'ridiculous parties' organised by people who were 'too full of their own importance'. Sarah knew that Gerald Compton's remarks about her slipping back into retirement hadn't helped. Tom wanted exactly that.

'I hope you'll be tendering for the work on the Deacon Estate, Sarah?'

Sarah turned her attention to Jim Stevens.

'Yes, it's all in hand. How many more houses are the council building up there?'

'Another forty. The rest of the land has been bought up by private developers . . . '

An hour or so later, Sarah and Tom returned to the yard, just in time to see a delivery van driving away.

'I wonder what — '

'I expect it's my desk,' Sarah murmured, getting out of the car.

'Desk?' Tom's puzzled expression turned to a thunderous scowl. 'And where do you imagine your desk is going? In my office?'

'*Our* office, Tom,' Sarah said firmly, trying to quell her nerves. She didn't want a confrontation over any of this.

Tom strode towards the office, Sarah following at a more sensible pace.

'How was the party?' Linda greeted them.

'A complete and utter waste of time,' Tom grumbled.

'A highly enjoyable public relations exercise,' Sarah said calmly. 'Was that my desk being delivered, Linda?'

'Yes. The keys are in the top drawer.'

They both went into their office. Sarah

grimaced when she saw that Tom's desk had been pushed back so that her own could sit in front of the window.

'There isn't room to swing a cat!' Tom exploded.

'I don't know about you but I have no intention of swinging cats.' Sarah tried to make light of it. 'I think it's quite cosy.'

Tom went and sat behind his desk.

'This is ridiculous,' he said at last. 'I'm not saying you haven't done a good job while I've been away but — '

'I should hope not!'

'But now I'm back — I know how things are run around here.'

'So do I.' Sarah caught his gaze and held it. 'This is *our* business, Tom. Yours and mine. I'm not a sleeping partner any longer.'

'Sarah — ' Tom took a deep breath, and struggled to keep his temper. 'There's no need for you to do anything.'

'There's every need.' Sarah chose her words with great care. 'I know you're back to full strength, but you're not getting any younger, Tom. With both of us working together — '

'As in 'too many cooks spoil the broth'?' Tom demanded.

'No. As in 'many hands make light work'.'

236

'It won't work, Sarah!' he exploded.

'Because you don't want it to work!'

'You're right. I don't!'

'But I do. I'm not having you working yourself straight back into hospital, Tom,' Sarah said quietly. 'I know what I'm doing here. I've built up some useful contacts and suppliers. And now that the children are leading their own lives, there's little for me to do at home. I need something else. I need to feel useful.'

'Then get a job,' Tom said. 'I've nothing against you working, Sarah. Something secretarial, perhaps?'

Sarah felt a sudden urge to hit him.

'I don't want something secretarial. I'm too good for that.'

'But you don't know the first thing about — Oh, I know all about the golf club. I've heard nothing else all afternoon, but that was only one job, Sarah. I won't call it luck but — '

'Luck?' Sarah fumed. 'Don't you dare, Tom! If there was any luck involved, all of it was bad. Everything that could go wrong, did, and we still got the job finished. If it wasn't for me, you'd have nothing left!'

'All right. All right. You did a good job and I'm proud of you, really I am. But now we can get back to normal.'

The phone rang and he picked it up. His lips thinned.

'It's for you.' He handed the receiver to Sarah.

As Sarah took the call, she thought that in almost thirty years of marriage, she had never seen a sneer like that on Tom's face. And she hoped she never saw it again. She wondered, too, when she had last seen Tom smile. Certainly not since he'd come out of hospital, and realised that life had changed. That they had changed.

★ ★ ★

'My father will be here at twelve,' Nigel Emmerson reminded Cassie for the umpteenth time. 'I hope everything goes all right. We'll have lunch first, shall we? Or should we have lunch later?'

Cassie felt like screaming. She was attempting, for the third time, to add a column of figures.

'It might be better to have lunch later,' Nigel went on, 'when we've had a chance to discuss it all. On the other hand, if he hasn't eaten —'

'For goodness' sake!' Cassie spun round in her chair to face him. 'Am I missing something here, Nigel? Is it just your father

238

coming, or is he bringing the Queen with him?'

'I just want everything to go off all right,' Nigel murmured. 'What do you think? Do we eat first or leave it till later?'

'Eat first,' Cassie replied, not bothering to give the matter any thought.

'Right.'

Nigel drummed his fingers on the edge of his desk and Cassie silently counted to ten. She would have been amused if it hadn't been so annoying. Where was his cool exterior now?

'Don't expect the fact that he's my father to count for anything,' Nigel said. 'That just makes him worse. We certainly won't be granted any favours.'

'Aren't you close?' Cassie asked curiously, and Nigel thought for a moment.

'I suppose we are, for Christmas, weddings and christenings and that sort of thing. But when it comes to business — he expects everything to be perfect, you see.'

Like someone else I know, Cassie thought with amusement.

'Don't worry, Nigel. Gary's promised not to serve the soup in his lap.'

'Don't!' Nigel closed his eyes.

'It's just a flying visit,' Cassie said patiently. 'He'll only be here for — what — five hours?'

Nigel grimaced.

'He can wreak havoc in five hours.'

With a chuckle, Cassie turned back to her column of figures.

She thought of Ian's letter, which she'd been carrying around for almost a week. She'd vowed to find five minutes during the morning to write a quick reply. There was no chance today, though.

I still feel the same, Ian had written. *I hope you do, too.*

She did feel the same. She just couldn't seem to find the time to tell him so.

She turned her attention back to her figures and was just making a note of the total when the phone rang.

'Mr Emmerson's car is just drawing up,' said a breathless voice from Reception.

Cassie wasn't sure what to expect by the time Nigel came back with his father. What she found was a man who was friendly, charming and witty.

He was also a very shrewd businessman. Even as he was relating some anecdote over lunch, Cassie was aware that his eyes were everywhere. Like Nigel, he was very watchful.

Looking at the two of them, she could detect a slight resemblance, but listening to them, no one would have guessed they were father and son. This was purely business.

Later, Cassie saw other similarities. Both were stubborn. Both were razor sharp. And both had been given calculators for brains.

'You could easily have gone for another few rooms in the new complex,' Charles Emmerson suggested.

'It wasn't feasible,' Nigel argued. 'We considered it, naturally, but it would have meant cutting back on the leisure complex.'

'Is that so important?' his father asked. 'Surely space could have been saved on the swimming pool and sauna, for instance.'

'Not really. There are several places locally where good rooms can be found, but we'll be the only one to cater for conferences. To do that we need the best technology and a first-class leisure complex.'

'How about parking?'

'We've decided it's adequate,' Cassie said. 'If every guest wanted parking facilities, we'd be struggling, but they don't.'

'Car hire?'

'No problems there,' Nigel assured him.

'We've also come to an arrangement with the estate nearby so that we can cater for fishing parties,' Cassie added, and a sudden thought struck her. 'I don't suppose you know the area too well, Mr Emmerson. Perhaps you have time for a quick tour?'

He checked his watch, and then looked up,

smiling. 'Yes. Splendid idea.'

Cassie was almost overwhelmed with relief. Nigel, who'd given every appearance of taking the cross-examination in his stride, seemed equally relieved to exchange the office for the watery sunshine.

They gave Charles Emmerson a rushed tour of the area, stopping to show him the local beauty spots and the two golf courses, before returning to the hotel. By then, it was time for their guest to leave.

'Thank goodness that's over,' Nigel said, as they walked slowly back to their office.

'I think he was quite impressed,' Cassie remarked.

'I think he was very impressed,' Nigel agreed. 'Thanks for your help, Cassie. Let's call it a day and get something to eat.'

Cassie thought of the busy restaurant and shook her head. It had been a long day and she wanted peace and quiet.

'We don't have to eat here,' Nigel said. 'We could try out the opposition.'

That sounded even worse. On the other hand, left to her own devices she would have to sit down and answer Ian's letter and she wasn't in the mood.

'How about a picnic?' she suggested.

'Fine,' Nigel said, bemused. The idea would obviously never have occurred to him.

'I'll go and see what I can scrounge in the kitchen.'

The kitchen was between busy periods and the staff were enjoying a gossip until Cassie walked in. She'd noticed several times lately how conversations stopped abruptly when she ventured within earshot. She had always been privy to the grapevine but now she supposed they thought of her as being on the other side of the fence.

Having sorted out their food and chosen a bottle of white wine to accompany it, Cassie returned to her office with a vague feeling of depression.

Nigel drove them out to Glengarry Hill, where the lights of the hotel were part of a twinkling mass below. It was cold, and darkness was already beginning to close in, but they braved the elements to enjoy their food.

Cassie was subdued, and Nigel had the wit to notice.

'What happened in the kitchen?' he asked.

'Nothing.' Cassie smiled briefly. 'I'm probably peeved because I'm missing out on the gossip.'

Nigel gave her a long, considering look. 'Nowadays you are the gossip.'

'Me?'

'Hawk-eye's sidekick.' Nigel laughed at her

outraged expression. 'They're your friends, but it's human nature to wonder how you got the job, and perhaps wait for you to fall flat on your face. Besides, when two people share an office, there's always a certain amount of speculation, isn't there?'

Cassie's eyes widened. People surely didn't think that she and Nigel — but no, they knew her too well. Most of them knew Ian, too. And Ian and Nigel were as different as two men could be . . .

'You'll have to learn to live with it,' Nigel told her firmly. 'I can't afford to lose you. We make a good team.'

That surprised Cassie. At first, she'd concentrated on getting through each day without making any mistakes. Then, when she realised that she was good at the job, she'd started to relax.

Nigel was right though. There was more to it than that. They worked well together, compensating for each other's weaknesses.

Nigel was the one who made the decisions, who came up with the ideas, and kept them on top of things. Cassie got the most out of people, spotted potential problems, and helped to keep Nigel's feet on the ground.

She'd never thought about it before but it was very much a two-way relationship. And tonight, she realised for the first time that it was beginning to extend beyond the office.

'To us.' Nigel lifted his glass.

Cassie slowly touched her glass against his. 'To us,' she murmured.

11

'We used to relax on Sundays,' Tom muttered. 'We used to do things together.'

Sarah, on her way to the kitchen, suppressed a sigh.

'I won't be long,' she promised. 'It's just a few cakes for the church coffee morning.'

'I don't know why you have to take so much on,' Tom grumbled. 'You don't have time for your own family, so why worry about coffee mornings?'

'I have all the time in the world for my family,' Sarah said. 'And baking a few cakes can hardly be termed as taking a lot on.'

'It can when you've been working all week.' Tom rounded on her. 'It can when we arrive home, as we did last night, to find our daughter looking for something that might make a half decent meal!'

'Oh really, Tom, Helen's quite capable. And since when have you kicked up a fuss just because there hasn't been a meal waiting on the table?'

He scowled at her.

'I'm going into the garden.'

Sarah flinched as the back door slammed.

Naively, she'd imaged that once Tom had got used to the idea of her working alongside him, things would improve between them. Instead their relationship, both at work and at home, had gone from bad to worse.

It wasn't that they argued exactly. It was just that this wall between them seemed to grow higher by the day. Throughout their marriage, they had never been so unable — or so unwilling — to communicate. Their marriage used to be a wealth of affection glances, understanding smiles, and loving gestures . . .

Sarah was about to start on her cakes when Matthew and Kerry called.

'Is Uncle Tom in the garden?' Kerry complained. 'He didn't tell me!'

'He's only just gone outside,' Sarah assured her with a smile. 'He's probably seeing if he can find some work for you.'

Kerry skipped out to join him, and Sarah felt her heart tug at the smile Tom gave the little girl.

'Is Helen in?' Matthew asked.

'No. She and Joe are out at the cottage, painting their kitchen. Was it important?'

'She said she might be able to have Kerry on Wednesday afternoon,' Matthew explained. 'I've got to meet my agent, and Helen thought Kerry might like to 'help out' at the shop for a couple of hours. I wanted to check that it was OK.'

'I'm sure it will be. Helen loves having Kerry around. I'll tell her — Now, are you stopping for a cup of tea? I know I could do with one.'

Matthew glanced out of the window to where Kerry and Tom were digging in a flower bed. 'I'd love one, thanks.'

Sarah thought of calling Tom in, but decided against it. He'd be far happier with Kerry.

'How's Cassie?' Matthew asked. 'I haven't seen her for ages.'

'I've hardly seen her myself.' Sarah laughed. 'She's working hard again. And thriving on it.'

'Tom's looking better than ever.'

Tom did look well. Physically, he was back to his old self again. It was just as well, Sarah thought. Her working alongside him was supposed to lighten his burden, but all it was doing was aggravating him. She was convinced that, in the long run, she was right to stick it out. But would giving in be better for his peace of mind?

'Problems?' Matthew noted her thoughtful expression.

'Nothing we can't handle,' she said quietly. 'After almost thirty years of marriage, I've just learned that Tom is a male chauvinist. He likes the idea of his wife being at home with a meal and slippers at the ready!'

'We're all guilty of that.' Matthew chuckled. 'We have every respect for career women, but there's nothing to beat coming home to a wife who'll listen to our problems and cosset us.'

'I suppose so,' Sarah agreed. 'Working in the same office is bound to cause friction, too. Although Helen and Joe seem to manage perfectly well.'

'They're not married yet. Not that I can imagine Helen and Joe ever having an argument,' Matthew added quickly. 'Joe dotes on her too much. Quite right, too.'

His face was fleetingly wistful.

'Matthew,' Sarah began hesitantly, 'you and Helen — it was never — ?'

'No,' Matthew interrupted. 'Helen and I weren't right for each other. I wish things could have been different. But no, I wish them both every happiness. And I know they *will* be happy.'

'I'm sure they will.' Sarah agreed.

Tom and Kerry came in just then. Tom was his normal friendly self, thank goodness, and the Andersons stayed for almost an hour.

'I'll come tomorrow,' Kerry promised as they were leaving, 'and we'll have that bonfire. You won't forget, will you, Tom?'

'I won't forget, sweetheart,' Tom assured her, hugging her briefly. 'Just make sure you're wearing old clothes, otherwise we'll both be in trouble.'

Laughing, casual remarks, and only Sarah saw the pain in Tom's eyes as he waved the little girl away. Tom adored Kerry, they all did, but not even Kerry could make up for the loss of their own grandson.

'We have to look on the bright side, Tom,' Sarah said gently as she shut the door. 'Paul and Melanie are OK, and their marriage is stronger than it's ever been. And we've got Joe and Helen's wedding to look forward to.'

'You're not telling me anything I don't know.'

'But what I mean is, we'll have more grandchildren.'

Tom looked at her for a long time.

'All the grandchildren in the world won't bring little Thomas back.'

'It hurts me too, Tom.' Sarah longed for a word or a touch — anything.

'I know,' he answered with a sigh. 'And I wish there was something I could do or say that would help. But I can't talk to you, Sarah. You've changed. You're like a stranger to me.'

'If I have changed, it's because I've had to,' Sarah cried. 'I thought you might die, Tom.

Can you imagine how that felt? Half of me knew I couldn't cope without you, and the other half knew that I might have to. I'd spent years leaning on you and suddenly, you weren't there to lean on. I had to change to survive.'

'But that's over,' he said fiercely. 'The only thing that kept me sane in hospital was the thought of coming home to you. To the woman I loved, the woman who needed me, who relied on me. The woman who made me feel as if I was a real somebody.'

There was anguish in his eyes.

'You're not the woman I married, Sarah!'

★   ★   ★

Helen was pleased to see that Joe had finished painting the door in the hall, but after today, even the sight of her future home didn't cheer her.

She'd thought there could be nothing easier than going into a bridal shop and choosing a dress. All she wanted was something very simple in design, but that, it seemed, was impossible.

'Bad day?' Joe guessed.

'Disastrous!'

'There's plenty of time,' he soothed.

'That's just it, Joe, there isn't. Time's

251

running out fast. I wish now we'd gone to the Registrar.'

'No you don't.' Joe put his brush down. 'You wanted all the trimmings — a day to look back on. Remember?'

'That was before I knew how much was involved. I'm dreading it, Joe. I'll look like a ghost. Added to that, there are sure to be dozens of people we've forgotten to invite. The photographer probably won't turn up. The cake will be — '

'Helen, calm down!' He came over to take her in his arms. 'Weddings are always chaotic, you know they are.'

Helen was dangerously close to tears.

'Melanie's wasn't like this.'

'I expect it was.' Joe smiled.

'It's all right for you. All you have to do is turn up at the right time!' Helen's voice rose. 'And I had your mother on the phone three times this morning.'

'Three?'

'Three! First to ask what colour Mum's wearing, then to make sure we didn't forget to invite your Aunt Sophie. And the third call was to warn us that if Aunt Sophie turned up, she and Uncle George would spend the duration pointedly ignoring each other.'

'Mum doesn't know what she's wearing, any more than I do.' Helen sighed. 'Although we have decided on blue for the bridesmaids.'

'I thought it was going to be peach,' Joe said, puzzled.

'It was, but now it's blue. I'm sure I would have got on better on my own. Melanie wanted frills and bows and Cassie — well, she was in a most peculiar mood!'

'Is all of this really getting you down, Helen?'

Joe looked so concerned that she wished she could shrug it all off, but she couldn't. She'd begun to wonder if she'd have enough energy to raise a smile on the big day.

Joe kissed her hair.

'If everything went wrong, would it really be so terrible?'

'Yes!'

'No.' He smiled. 'What would it matter if the cars didn't arrive? Your dad would call a taxi or two, that's all. And if the photographer forgot to turn up, we'd have to make do with snaps taken by the guests.'

He held her close.

'Disaster or otherwise, Helen, we'll be walking out of the church as husband and wife. Surely that's what matters.'

Husband and wife!

Helen leaned against him and blinked back her tears. Joe was right. With so many things to think about, it was easy to forget the reason for all the fuss. The fact that they would be making vows to bind them together for the rest of their lives had somehow become a minor consideration.

'Sorry,' she murmured.

Joe kissed her.

'Everything will be fine, darling. You'll see.'

Of course it would, and Helen suddenly felt she'd been very childish.

'What I said about you only having to turn up at the right time — I know you're doing everything you can to help, and I'm sorry.'

'I should think so,' he replied with a mock scowl. 'I have the honeymoon to worry about!'

'If you'd just give me a clue,' Helen coaxed and Joe laughed.

'I told you that it should be warm, and you know I've got your passport. That's enough clues.'

'But how warm is warm? Just tell me roughly how long it takes to get there. We do go on a plane, don't we? Because I hate boats . . .'

Joe silenced her questions with another kiss.

★ ★ ★

Sitting on the plane to London, Cassie went over and over what she was going to say to Ian. When she wasn't doing that, she was remembering all the good times they'd had.

She'd started several letters to him, but she couldn't put her feelings into words. And Ian deserved more than a letter.

If she hadn't had that day out with her sisters, helping to choose Helen's wedding dress, things would have been left to drift along. But that day, she'd spotted a dress hanging on its own, away from the main display.

It wouldn't have appealed to Helen, with its rows of tiny pearls on the sleeves, neckline and hem, but Cassie had fallen in love with it.

She'd closed her eyes and pictured herself walking down the aisle with the long train flowing behind her. She had seen it all so vividly.

Sunlight had been streaming through the church windows. The guests had fallen silent. She had seen the groom turn his head slightly. And then she had been looking straight into Nigel Emmerson's smiling face.

Nigel's. Not Ian's.

She should have known. Perhaps she had known . . . perhaps she just hadn't been able to face the truth.

For a few days after that she'd tried to

forget it all, in the hope that everything would sort itself out. But life wasn't like that.

So she had phoned Ian, and they had arranged to meet in London . . .

He was waiting for her at the airport and, as soon as she saw him, Cassie longed to get back on the plane without having to utter a word.

He took her in his arms and hugged her. He was so dear and so very familiar. And yet — different somehow.

They both started talking at once. Cassie was trying to behave normally — she couldn't tell him in the middle of a crowded airport terminal — but it was an impossible situation.

As they walked to his car, he didn't stop talking about the restaurant. Then, as they drove away, he fired questions at her about her job with the new conference centre. He wasn't giving her the chance to say anything.

'Shall we get some lunch?' he asked. 'You must be hungry.'

'Not The Highlander, Ian.' Food was the last thing on her mind.

'No,' he agreed. 'We'll go somewhere else.'

They lapsed into silence and just when Cassie had decided to lead up very gently to the reason for her visit, Ian stopped the car.

'It isn't far from here,' he explained.

As they walked the short distance to the restaurant, Cassie knew she wouldn't be able to tell him over lunch. It would have to wait until later.

At the door, he stopped. After gazing at her for a long time, he said quietly, 'I've lost you, haven't I?'

He knew, of course. He knew her better than anyone did, he always had.

'Ian, I'm sorry. I can't marry you. Not now. Not ever.' Tears filled her eyes as she said again, 'I'm so sorry.'

He had known, but he still looked terribly shaken. He tried to speak, then decided against it.

He opened the door, then hesitated again.

'Are you hungry?' he asked, and Cassie shook her head.

'Me neither,' he said.

He closed the door, took Cassie's hand and started walking along the street. He didn't speak.

Cassie had no idea where they were going. She doubted if Ian knew. He was holding her hand tightly, as if he had no intention of letting her go. Cassie wasn't sure that she wanted him to.

'Have you met someone else?' he asked at last.

She'd 'met' Nigel. But now Cassie knew

that, sooner or later, she would have reached this decision anyway. Her reluctance to marry Ian, her refusal to come to London with him — it all added up.

Her feelings for Nigel were very different from the way she had felt about Ian. Mentioning Nigel to Ian would only complicate the issue, Cassie felt. It would also hurt him even more and she couldn't bear to do that.

'No, there's no one else,' she said softly.

'Then why?' Ian demanded. 'All these years — '

'Perhaps that's it,' Cassie said quietly. 'Perhaps we became a habit?'

'A habit?' he echoed incredulously.

'I didn't mean it like that!' Cassie groaned. 'I mean I've loved you since I was five years old. I love you now. But it's not the right kind of love, Ian. I love you as a friend, a brother almost.'

'Spare me that!'

They walked for what seemed like miles. Cassie's hand was still in his, and her legs ached from trying to keep up with his strides.

She wanted to make him understand, but she was afraid of making matters worse. She didn't love him enough, and she knew he didn't want to hear that, no matter how she dressed it up.

She realised that they'd walked a complete circle and were standing outside the restaurant again. Cassie still wasn't hungry, but she was glad to sit down and rest her feet.

When the food arrived, they were both relieved to be able to push it around their plates.

'I'd planned to take it very well,' Ian said, finally breaking the silence.

'How did you know what I was going to say?'

'From your phone call. I knew it wasn't good news. But I suppose I've known for a long time. It wasn't working, was it? Me down here, you up there.'

'It wasn't working before then,' Cassie said urgently. 'Not really.'

'Don't tell me it was just habit!' He sighed. 'What am I supposed to say?'

Cassie was silent.

'Is there anything I can say that will change your mind? Is there anything I can do? If I moved back — '

'No.'

'So what do you want to hear?' he demanded. 'Goodbye? Good luck? If you ever change your mind?'

Cassie hadn't expected him to look quite so lost. Beneath all the hurt, the frustration and the anger, he looked like a small boy.

'I'm sorry, Ian.'

'So you keep telling me.'

They finished their meal in silence and then left the restaurant.

Ian drove to Hyde Park, and they walked again. Cassie was relieved when it was time to return to the airport. She was pleased now that she'd decided on the shuttle. In a little more than two hours she would be home.

'There's no need to wait with me,' she told Ian awkwardly as they arrived at Heathrow.

'I'll wait,' he replied.

Cassie didn't know whether to be pleased or not. She knew she would breathe more easily when he'd gone, but she also knew that this was a turning point. The plane would take her to a new life, a life that didn't include Ian, and that seemed almost frightening.

Finally her flight was called. She turned to face Ian, but there wasn't a single word she could say. She kissed him very quickly and then started walking away.

It was all wrong. It was awful.

She turned around and ran back to him.

'You're the dearest friend I have in the world, Ian,' she said urgently. 'I couldn't bear to lose that friendship.'

He looked at her for so long that Cassie thought she had asked too much. Then he opened his arms and held her close. Too close — Cassie could feel him inwardly crying.

She pulled away from him and ran, before he could see the tears pouring down her own face.

★ ★ ★

Tom was furious. There was no other word for it. He had just found out, when it was common knowledge to everyone else, that they were way behind schedule on the Leonard's contract.

And how had he found out? Linda had mentioned it in passing, assuming, of course that he knew all about it.

He sat at his desk, fuming. When he heard a van pull into the yard he went to the window and looked out. Seeing that it was Alex, Tom strode outside.

'Alex!' he shouted across the yard. 'I want a word with you!'

Tom went back to his office, sat at his desk and waited. A full five minutes passed before his assistant strolled into the office, a fact that did nothing to improve Tom's temper.

'I hear we've got problems with the Leonard's Job.' He got straight to the point.

Alex nodded. 'That's right.'

'Why?'

'A combination of things,' Alex replied thoughtfully. 'The weather, materials not being delivered, other jobs being given priority.'

'And you didn't think to tell me?' Tom thundered.

Alex gazed back at him.

'I told Sarah.'

'And all Sarah seems to have done is told Linda,' Tom said, his voice heavy with sarcasm. 'That's not the point, though, is it? Why the devil wasn't I told?'

'Sarah was the first person I saw,' Alex explained steadily. 'And I was under the impression that telling Sarah was the same as telling you. You are partners, after all.'

'Partners we might be but — '

'If you must know,' Alex interrupted him harshly, 'I prefer to deal with Sarah, and so does everyone else. You're so unpredictable these days, Tom, that nobody knows what to expect. Since you got back we all tip-toe around watching what we say. With Sarah, everyone knows where they stand.'

Tom was all set to give him a piece of his mind when the phone rang.

'Was there anything else?' Alex asked. 'I need to help unload a pile of timber. For Leonard's, as it happens.'

'Nothing that won't keep,' Tom muttered

furiously, reaching for the telephone.

When he'd finished the call, he sat back in his chair and went over every word that Alex had said. Unpredictable. That was exactly how Sarah had described him.

Was he unpredictable?

He hadn't been in the best of tempers lately, admittedly, but who would be? His life had been turned completely upside down. And how was he expected to behave when half the work force were bypassing him and going straight to his wife?

Were they going straight to Sarah because he was 'unpredictable'? Or was he unpredictable because half the time he didn't have a clue what was going on?

Just then he heard Sarah return. He could hear her voice in the outer office, chatting to Linda. He heard her burst of laughter, and felt suddenly chilled. It was a sound he had almost forgotten.

Seconds later, she walked in.

'Hello, Tom.'

They might have been casual acquaintances ... or business partners, he thought grimly.

He just looked at her. There was no laughter now, not even a smile. She looked wary, afraid of him almost. No, it wasn't fear. More like resignation. Or was it dread?

In that instant, Tom knew that she would rather have found the office empty. His own wife, and she wished him a hundred miles away!

'I — I — ' Tom cleared his throat and started again. 'Linda mentioned something about the Leonard's contract being behind schedule.'

'I've just come from there.' Sarah nodded. 'They aren't too worried. It's partly their fault for changing the plans.'

Exactly what Tom had wanted to say — if anyone had let him say anything on the subject.

'I told them we'd be finished in a month,' Sarah explained. 'That gives us more than enough time, and they're happy enough.'

Tom watched her sit at her desk. She put her papers in a neat pile in front of her, then, with notepad and pencil at the ready, made three telephone calls. With those out of the way, she made copious notes, and then checked, very carefully, a detailed invoice.

'Sarah?'

She looked across at him, that wary look back in her eyes.

'I — nothing,' Tom murmured. 'It'll keep. I'm going out.'

'Oh?' She was relieved. 'Where?'

Tom didn't have a clue.

'I won't be late. I'll go straight home.'

He left the office, got into his car and drove. He had no idea where he was going; he just knew that he couldn't have stayed in that office a moment longer. He couldn't bear the way Sarah looked at him.

Driving into town, he found the nearest car park and decided to walk off his frustration.

Like it or not, he'd come to accept that Sarah was in his office to stay. Now he came to think about it, he wasn't sure what he disliked the most. Helen had accused him of being old-fashioned enough to want his wife tied to the kitchen sink, but it wasn't that.

Tom stopped to admire some red roses in the florist's window and wondered who would be fool enough to pay such a price for them. Despite the price, though, he felt a sudden urge to buy them for Sarah.

He walked on. It would take more than roses to put things right between them. Anyway, she wouldn't have liked them, would she? It was the wrong time of year for roses . . .

All the same, he would have liked to take something home, to see Sarah smile, to take her in his arms, to be her husband again . . .

Perhaps, a tiny voice prompted, it was Sarah's success at the yard that he resented. But surely he wasn't that petty . . .

He turned around and walked slowly back towards the florist's. They would have other flowers inside the shop, ones that Sarah *would* like. If he didn't know what she liked after thirty years of marriage, there was little hope for them.

He took a deep breath and walked into the shop. He didn't know what Sarah's reaction would be. He just knew that he had to do something. And this had to be a step in the right direction.

12

'Would you like a coffee?' Cassie asked Nigel.

'I don't have the time. In case you've forgotten,' he added drily, 'I've got a plane to catch.'

Cassie mumbled something appropriate and carried on working. Nigel was in a strange mood, had been all week. Perhaps on Monday, he would be in a better frame of mind.

There was nothing at work bothering him, at least she couldn't think of anything. So it had to be something personal. And when it came to his personal life, she was at a loss.

It had to be said that he couldn't have much of a personal life, because he was too involved with the hotel. She knew he often played squash, but if he had a free weekend, he usually went down south to his parents' home.

Cassie's telephone rang and she switched her thoughts back to business as she picked it up.

'You're sounding very efficient,' Ian's voice greeted her.

'Naturally!' Cassie laughed. 'How are you, Ian?'

'Fine. I'll be up for a few days with Mum and Dad next week. I wondered if we could have lunch or something.'

Cassie frowned. She'd spoken to Ian three times since her visit to London and, although each time had been easier than the last, and he seemed now to have accepted the situation, she wasn't sure they were ready to have lunch together.

'And I thought I was the dearest friend you had,' Ian teased, sensing her hesitation.

'You are. It's just that — '

'Would it make any difference if I told you I'd met someone else?' Ian said calmly.

Cassie was delighted, and relieved.

'Well, of course. That changes everything. Ian, I'm so pleased.'

The silence was confusing, then Cassie realised what was going on.

'You haven't met anyone, have you?'

'Not yet, but I'm prepared to lie a little.'

A reluctant smile brightened Cassie's face. Ian wasn't going to make it difficult. He'd accepted her decision, and was merely offering friendship. She didn't want to lose that, they'd shared far too much over the years. They had to meet one day and it may as well be sooner . . .

'OK, thanks. Give me a ring when you get here. I'll look forward to it.'

When Cassie replaced the receiver, Nigel slammed his briefcase shut and got to his feet. 'So is this on or off?' he demanded.

His anger confused Cassie. She'd had the feeling for weeks that she'd done something wrong. She just wished Nigel would tell her what it was.

'Is what on or off?'

'The big romance,' he replied sarcastically. 'Six weeks ago, it was all over the hotel that it was off. Now, by the sound of it, it's back on.'

Nigel was clearly spoiling for a fight.

'I don't see that it's any business of yours,' she snapped.

'If only that were true. Personally, I couldn't care less one way or the other, but I might just point out that you're here to work.'

'What the devil do you think I've been doing?' Cassie retorted.

'Moping about your love life!' He stood in front of her desk. 'I've been patient, heaven knows, but there are limits. You're paid to work. If you can't manage that, I suggest you write out your resignation.'

Cassie, too shocked to say anything, watched him slam out of the office.

She reached for a pen, grabbed a piece of paper and started to write: *Dear Mr*

Emmerson, Please accept this as notification —

She screwed the paper into a ball and hurled it at the wastepaper basket.

Once she'd calmed down a little, she made herself a coffee and sat at Nigel's desk to drink it. She often used his desk when he wasn't there. For one thing, his chair was much better than hers. Both were sold as 'executive' chairs but his was far more executive than hers. It was high-backed and made of soft, unbelievably comfortable Italian leather.

Unfortunately, Cassie was in no mood to appreciate it.

What angered her most was the way he'd left her no chance to defend herself. If he'd wanted to find fault with her work, he might at least have the decency to do so in a calm, rational manner. But that was typical of Nigel. He was totally lacking in tact, which was why he'd had Jeannie McInnes in tears within hours of his arrival.

Well, he wouldn't reduce Cassie to tears, nor would he persuade her to offer her resignation. If he wanted to get rid of her, he'd have a fight on his hands.

What if he really did want to get rid of her? Cassie wondered suddenly. What would she do if she lost this job? More importantly, what would she do if she couldn't see Nigel every day?

Her thoughts chased themselves in circles as she drank her coffee. Only reluctantly did she allow the truth to surface.

The truth was that Nigel was right. She hadn't been pulling her weight lately.

Her lack of concentration couldn't be blamed on her friendship with Ian, though. She'd been upset, of course, but it was the right decision.

If there had been any loss of concentration, and she had to admit that there had, it was because she was finding it almost impossible to keep her mind off Nigel.

The sound of his voice fascinated her. His hair fascinated her, and the way that he always had it cut just when she noticed that it had a tendency to curl. One day, she'd been so engrossed by the pattern on his tie that she hadn't heard half of what he was saying to her . . .

Her sense of humour returned and she chuckled to herself. She was behaving like a twelve-year-old.

She took a piece of paper from his jotter and, in large black letters, wrote:

Sorry. She propped it against his phone.

Somehow, she had to get their relationship

back to the way it had been. They'd got on so well.

On Monday, she would apologise for her lapses of concentration and show Nigel that she was the best person for the job.

Meanwhile, she would go home and forget his parting words.

She arrived home at the same time as Helen.

'I'll be walking down the aisle in a pair of jeans!' her sister wailed.

'Whatever's happened?' Cassie asked.

'I was supposed to go and collect the dress today, but they rang to say it's not finished.'

Before Cassie could sympathise, Helen added, 'The invitations have gone out today. I bet we've forgotten someone.'

'I'm sure we — ' Cassie began, but Helen was already racing up the stairs.

Cassie was still taking off her coat when the phone rang.

'Cassie, it's me,' Melanie said. 'Is Mum there?'

'I've only just come in but her car's here. Just a minute — '

'No,' Melanie said quickly. 'Is Dad there, too?'

Cassie listened and heard him talking to Helen. 'Yes.'

'Don't tell them I rang,' Melanie said.

'We've got some news — we'll call round and surprise them. See you in about fifteen minutes.'

Cassie was still trying to guess what Melanie's news could be when she collided headon with her father.

'Cassie!' Tom drew back in dismay.

She stared at the broken stems that dangled from Tom's hands, and the petals scattered around their feet.

'Flowers?' she said in amazement.

'That's how they started the day,' Tom retorted drily.

'For Mum?' Cassie couldn't keep the astonishment from her voice. It had been a long time since Tom had come home with flowers, and now she'd spoiled it.

'Who else would they be for?' Tom asked with exasperation. 'Although I can't give her them now, can I? They were smashing, too!'

'I'm sorry, Dad.'

'Talk about clumsy.' A rueful smile hovered on his lips. 'Heaven knows where you inherited that from!'

Sarah came into the hall, and stopped when she saw them both. Her eyebrows rose slightly as she noticed the petals on the carpet.

With an exaggerated bow, Tom thrust the

remains of the flowers at her. 'For my wife. A small — and somewhat battered — token of my affection.'

Cassie slipped quietly upstairs.

Tom held his breath as Sarah took the flowers. A yellow bloom fell to the floor.

'Tom, they're — ' Words failed her as she gazed at them.

He watched her face. The smile barely touched her mouth, but it was there in her eyes, and it seemed to light up her whole face. It was a smile that said 'everything's all right', a smile that he'd taken for granted — until recently.

'They're truly beautiful, Tom!'

With a sudden burst of laughter, Sarah threw her arms around him, subjecting the flowers to more rough treatment in the process.

'They were,' he said with a smile. 'It took me ages to choose them, too.'

Hugging him, Sarah laughed until she cried.

She put her flowers in water and gave them pride of place in the sitting-room. They weren't much to look at, admittedly, but none had ever meant more to her.

As she was admiring them, Tom moved to stand behind her. He slipped his arms around her waist.

Sarah turned around, her eyes shadowed with doubts.

'Tom, will everything be all right? Us, I mean? Me working with you . . . ?'

'Everything will be fine,' he promised, bending his head to kiss her. 'I can't honestly say that I like the idea of you working alongside me, and I doubt if I ever will, but I'm prepared to give it a try. I'll admit that the idea has some advantages and I'll also admit that I've been the one making difficulties.'

'No, we've both been stubborn, Tom.'

'Perhaps. But let's put it behind us. It's time to put our priorities in order. The business is just a means of keeping body and soul together — it should never come between us. I should never have let it. You come first with me, Sarah, you always have and you always will. You, our marriage, our children.'

It was like welcoming back an old and very dear friend. This was her Tom, the man who, above all else, was a loving, family man.

Tom kissed her again. 'Why don't we — '

The front door crashed open.

'It's only us!' Melanie called out.

'In here, love,' Sarah replied.

'There's never a moment's peace in this place,' Tom grumbled, but his smile took the

275

sting from his words.

Paul and Melanie walked into the sitting-room with beaming smiles. Cassie and Helen, clearly forewarned, followed them. Sarah noted the concern on their faces and knew how they felt. Surprise visits, the ridiculous smiles — it could only mean one thing. Paul had dreamt up another of his crazy schemes. He was tired of the video shop already, and just when it looked like turning into a nice little business.

'This is a nice surprise,' she said carefully.

Like a magician pulling a rabbit from a hat, Paul produced a bottle of champagne, and Sarah's spirits sank even lower.

'Come on then!' Cassie burst out. 'Don't keep us in suspense!'

Melanie grasped Paul's hand tightly. She looks radiant, Sarah realised. Despite her doubts about Paul, she had to admit that she had never seen Melanie look happier — or more attractive.

'I'm pregnant!' Melanie said quietly, but there was no mistaking the joy in her voice.

Sarah gasped.

'Pregnant?' Tom repeated in amazement. 'You mean you're having a baby?'

A roar of laughter followed his words.

Sarah's laughter turned to tears as she hugged Melanie tight.

'I'm so proud of you, Melanie.' She held her daughter at arm's length. 'And I've never seen you look happier.'

'I've never been happier, Mum.'

Sarah had to wait her turn to congratulate Paul. What an unruly mob we are, she thought with amusement. Whenever there was cause for celebration, the family seemed to double in size. There were only six people in the room, but there might have been twenty.

Helen dashed to the telephone to call Joe, and minutes later, he joined them.

Everyone chatted and laughed, and Sarah kept herself a little apart from it all. Having the family all together, with not a sad thought between them, was more than enough for Sarah. It didn't seem long ago that she had wondered if they would ever know happiness again. And look at them now . . .

It was late when Tom and Sarah finally climbed into bed. Then, instead of lying in those barren silences that had become so frequent, they talked and talked. Throughout their marriage, this had been the most precious part of Sarah's day. When the house was quiet, they had always shared their every thought.

'What a day of surprises,' Sarah said happily. 'And without your flowers, Tom, it wouldn't have been half as exciting. That's what I've missed most, not being able to share everything with you.'

'I've missed that, too.'

'I knew that one of us had to make the first move, and I did try. But — well, I just didn't know where to start.'

'Neither did I,' Tom admitted. 'I couldn't decide whether to get those flowers or not. I thought you might hurl them back at me. I knew it was going to take a lot more than a bunch of flowers to put things right.'

Sarah laughed again at the memory.

'Seeing you with those poor flowers — I found myself looking straight at the man I married.'

'Sarah, before Melanie and Paul arrived — '

'Oh, yes,' Sarah remembered. 'You were about to ask me something.'

'I was going to suggest a holiday,' Tom said. 'Nothing fancy. The Lake District perhaps. Or Devon, or Cornwall.'

'But the wedding, Tom! We can't just take off on holiday.'

'Why not? The wedding's weeks away. And there's nothing much left to do.'

Sarah chuckled. There were a million and one things to do!

'Besides,' Tom went on, 'Helen and Joe

know what they're doing. With so much to think about, they'll probably be glad to see the back of us. Anyway, we can't live our lives around the children, Sarah. They've got their own lives now.'

'It's a nice idea, Tom.' Sarah said wistfully, 'but I'm not sure the timing's right.'

'The timing's perfect,' Tom argued firmly. 'We'll give Helen and Joe a bit of peace. Melanie and Paul are so wrapped up in themselves they won't notice we've gone. And Cassie's hardly ever home.'

'But the business — '

'Will take care of itself. It survived for months without me.' A note of amusement crept into his voice. 'I appreciate that it'll be touch and go, but it should just about manage without you for ten days or so.'

His arms tightened around her.

'We're the ones who need time together, Sarah,' he said softly. 'We've been through a lot — and none of it good. We need time alone, just the two of us.'

Sarah knew he was right.

'A second honeymoon?' he coaxed.

Sarah laughed.

'The Lakes,' she decided impulsively. 'That way, we'll be closer to home . . . '

They lay in silence for a while.

'Do you remember the first time we went

there?' Sarah asked suddenly. 'Before we were married?'

Tom chuckled.

'How could I forget? I've still got the rust marks.'

'It rained solid.'

'Every day.'

'Until the morning we left,' Sarah remembered. 'And then there was the time we took Helen — remember?'

'I remember, Sarah.'

★   ★   ★

When Cassie arrived at the hotel on Monday, the office she shared with Nigel was empty. Usually he was there waiting for her. Her message was still on his desk so she assumed he hadn't been in.

Over the weekend she'd managed to convince herself that a quick apology would put everything right. Now she wasn't so sure. Perhaps Nigel really was dissatisfied with her work? Perhaps he really did believe that the arrangement wasn't working.

Cassie pushed her thoughts aside and started work.

She was on the phone when he arrived. It was a difficult call from a Swedish company, and Cassie was grateful that the connection was only slightly better than the secretary's English.

Apart from noticing that he looked tired, Cassie's mind was too full to dwell on Nigel. She did see the half smile on his face as he saw her message, though.

The call ended and she waited for him to speak. He didn't.

'Good weekend?' she asked, deciding to forget all about Friday's quarrel.

'Hectic,' he replied. 'You?'

'Lovely, thanks.' She was about to tell him Melanie's news but changed her mind. She was too unsure of him. 'It was nice to relax for a while,' she said instead.

'About Friday,' he said abruptly. 'I'm sorry. I had no right to say what I did. Put it down to pressure of work and my usual lack of tact.'

'No, you were right. I haven't been pulling my weight lately.'

'I'm glad I didn't arrive to find your resignation waiting for me.' He smiled, but it was clearly an effort.

'There's no danger of that,' Cassie replied lightly.

'I do appreciate all you've done here — all you're doing,' Nigel went on. He sounded as if he had been rehearsing this speech all weekend. 'I realise that you're working far more hours than you should be.

And — I appreciate it.'

Cassie didn't know what to say. For some reason, she felt more uncomfortable than she had when he'd been shouting at her on Friday.

'Just to set the record straight,' she began awkwardly, 'the hotel gossip was correct. About Ian, I mean. It's all over. We still keep in touch, of course, and I hope we'll always be friends, but we decided to call it a day. I know you said you weren't interested but — in case there's any more speculation, I thought you should know the truth.'

'Thank you.' He nodded curtly.

The atmosphere was becoming unbearable and Cassie had to keep talking. 'You were right, I did have things on my mind. But it was nothing to do with Ian.'

Nigel frowned. 'Do you have problems? Anything I can help with?'

You could care, she thought wistfully. But he did care, she could see that.

'No,' she said quickly to cover her confusion. 'Thanks, but everything's sorted itself out now.'

Nigel's telephone rang and he lifted it with obvious relief. Then Cassie's telephone rang. Business as usual, and nothing had improved.

As the morning progressed, Cassie's vow not to think about Nigel and to concentrate on her work, was proving difficult. Every so often he sighed loudly. Then he started to tap his fingers on his desk until Cassie wanted to scream. Thank goodness it would soon be lunchtime.

Then Nigel was silent, and somehow that was even more distracting than the sighing.

She swivelled in her chair to look at him. He was sitting back, with his hands linked behind his head, watching her. He wasn't even pretending to work.

'What's wrong, Nigel?' Cassie put down her pen.

'I don't know.' He sighed again. 'Perhaps it's me. Is it me, or is it becoming more and more impossible to work in this room?'

'Well — '

'You're right,' Nigel said, getting to his feet. 'It's me.'

He strode over to the window and stared out for a few moments before turning around to face her.

'I like things to be black or white,' he said. 'Clear cut. I like to know where I stand with people. And with you, Cassie, I don't know from one minute to the next . . . '

13

'I know I said I couldn't care less about you and Ian, Cassie,' Nigel said. 'That was a lie — I do care. I kept thinking —

'Well, we've been out a few times and — I know it was always business, but I sometimes thought — and that's the problem. You see?'

Cassie had the glorious feeling that she was beginning to see. Nigel, normally the articulate businessman, was finding it impossible to complete a simple sentence. His ears were turning pink with embarrassment, and she smiled.

'Yes, I suppose it is funny,' he said, as the pink quickly turned to crimson. 'Perhaps you should forget I said anything. I'm not very good at this sort of thing.'

Cassie smiled at him.

'You just need the practice. And if that was an invitation to lunch, I accept.'

He stared at her. 'It wasn't . . . but it could be.' His face cleared. 'Would you like to go out for lunch?'

'Yes, please.' Cassie laughed softly.

'With me?' He sounded stunned.

'Yes, please. Oh, Nigel! On Friday, all I

could think about was you having said that you couldn't care less. I'm glad you care because I care, too.'

'You do?'

'Very much. Everything started going wrong between Ian and me — well, a long time ago. When you and I have been out together, I've known it was only business but it's meant much more than that — '

Nigel came round the desk, swept her into his arms and kissed her.

'I wish you'd told me all this before,' he said, and he kissed her again.

'I wanted to,' Cassie admitted, 'but I wasn't sure — ' She leaned against him. 'Not about me, but about you. I don't know what you do when you're not here. You visit your parents — for all I know, you might have someone there. There might be dozens of eligible young women lined up . . . '

'Half a dozen at the most,' he said, laughing.

'Your parents might not like the idea of you getting involved with a glorified secretary. We're so different, Nigel. Think about it. Think about the public school — that enormous house you grew up in — you even have servants!'

'We do not have servants!'

'So who's Martha?' Cassie demanded. 'And

285

who's the man who's answered the phone on the two occasions I've called you there? The one who sounds suspiciously like a butler?'

'This isn't like you at all, Cassie.' He was puzzled, cupping her face in his hands.

'I just can't bear the thoughts of having all this snatched away from me,' she admitted shakily. 'I'd hate to see you go off with a Penelope Ponsonby-Smythe.'

Nigel grinned.

'It won't happen, darling. Look, I went to the same school as my father, simply because he thought it was a good school. The house is enormous, yes, but only because my mother had planned on having lots of children. After Caroline, though, she couldn't have any more. Anyway, it's a nice house. Martha helps every day with the cooking and cleaning — she's been there for as long as I can remember. And Jim, who sounds nothing like a butler, helps with all sorts of things. The garden, the weekly moving of furniture that my mother seems to insist on, driving — '

'Driving?'

'My mother doesn't drive,' Nigel explained. 'She works five mornings a week, running the local playgroup.' He grinned suddenly. 'She even gets paid for it!'

He tried to kiss her doubts away.

'You'll have to come home with me. You'll

like them. My father's a different person when he's away from work. Besides, you had him eating out of your hand when he came up to look round.'

His phone rang, and he kept one arm around Cassie as he reached for it. He listened carefully.

'My lunch appointment?' he said, amused. 'Oh my — '

Cassie's hands flew to her face. She'd made an appointment for him with Andrew Drayton. She'd left a note on his desk, which he obviously hadn't seen, and she'd forgotten to mention it.

His hand tightened playfully around Cassie's neck as he spoke, 'OK Diane. I'll be over there in two minutes . . . Yes, thanks.'

He put down the receiver.

'It looks as if we'll have to postpone our lunch date.'

'I left a note on your desk,' Cassie explained apologetically.

'I should have known it would be my fault!'

'Sorry, but I've had other things on my mind.' Cassie laughed. 'Andrew Drayton wanted to see you, and I thought he needed sweetening up a bit.' She gave him her most winning smile. 'And who better?'

'Don't make plans for this evening,' Nigel warned her. 'We'll have dinner with my mother. We can stay the night and drive back in time for the meeting tomorrow afternoon.'

Cassie was doubtful — and very nervous.

'It's very short notice, Nigel. Your mother — '

'Will be thrilled,' he finished for her, 'when I tell her I'm bringing the woman I intend to marry.'

Marry! Life was suddenly moving much too fast — but that was Nigel, Cassie supposed. Everything had to be done yesterday.

He was looking very sure of himself, too, she noticed.

'What happened to the man who could barely string two words together?' she asked.

'Isn't it amazing what the love of a good woman can do for a man?'

He straightened a perfectly straight tie, dropped a single kiss on her forehead, and headed for the door, just as Jeannie McInnes' came in.

'It's a glorious day, Jeannie!' Nigel greeted her.

Jeannie glanced at the windows to confirm that it was still pouring with rain, then gave Nigel a look that questioned his sanity.

'His Lordship's in a good mood,' Jeannie said when Nigel had gone. She didn't add 'for a change'.

'Beneath it all, Jeannie,' Cassie replied softly, 'there beats a heart of pure gold.'

Jeannie treated Cassie to the same look. 'I'll have to take your word for that!'

★ ★ ★

When Helen woke, it was several moments before she realised what day it was. She sprang out of bed and pulled back the curtains.

Already the sun was trying to shine, and a few white clouds ambled thoughtfully across a pale blue sky.

There was a quiet tap on her door.

'Helen? Are you awake?'

'Yes, Cassie.'

Her sister bounced into the room.

'How are you feeling?'

'Wonderful!' Helen pulled a face. 'And a little nervous.'

'Me too,' Cassie said.

Helen looked surprised.

'Not only do I have to perform my duties as bridesmaid,' Cassie told her, 'but the responsibility of the reception is on my shoulders, too.'

'By the time we get to the hotel, I'll be past caring,' Helen assured her. Her face softened. 'I wonder how Joe's feeling.'

'He's probably been camped out at the church all night.' Cassie grinned.

While Helen dutifully sat in bed waiting for her breakfast — Cassie's treat — she gazed fondly around her room. She remembered all the nights she'd spent here, studying hard to achieve her dream of going to university. Then once she'd got her place, she'd spent sleepless nights dreading a move away from home. It was strange to think that, if she hadn't made that move, if she'd read some other subject, she mightn't have met Joe . . .

'This is like those midnight feasts we used to have.' Cassie returned with the breakfasts. 'Remember?'

'All those biscuit crumbs and sticky sweet wrappers.' Helen smiled.

After their leisurely breakfast, the day began to quicken its pace.

There was a household of relatives to chat to, phone calls to take. In the midst of it all, Moira arrived to do Helen's hair, and Matthew brought Kerry.

Melanie arrived, the flowers were delivered, the bridesmaids were dressed. And Helen, suffering from a sudden bout of nerves, was finally helped into her dress.

'Why, Helen!' Sarah quickly reached for a tissue.

Melanie opened her mouth to speak, but

290

got no further than that. Even Cassie was at a loss for words.

'Helen!' Kerry cried, clapping her hands with delight. 'You look just like a princess. A real one!'

Helen looked to Sarah for reassurance, but her mother was too busy struggling with her tears to speak.

'Mum!' Helen laughed with exasperation. 'You've seen me in this dress half a dozen times.'

'I know, but not like this. I have never seen you look more beautiful — never imagined — ' Gulping back her tears, Sarah joked, 'It's just as well you girls get your looks from me!'

The house slowly emptied until only Helen and her father were left.

'I think this is where I'm supposed to say something really profound.' Tom said. 'And I can't think of a single thing!'

'I think it's all been said, Dad.' Helen laughed. 'Anyway, I couldn't cope with anything too profound at the moment.'

'Nervous?'

'A bit,' Helen admitted. 'All those people — '

'There's no need,' Tom said softly. 'This is your day, love. Yours and Joe's. The guests are grateful just to be able to share a little of it with you. And Joe — ' Tom had a faraway look in his eyes. 'He'll be overwhelmed by pride, happiness, and love. He'll remember today, and the way he felt when he saw his bride standing beside him, for the rest of his life.'

'There's experience talking,' Helen teased and her father nodded.

'I don't know what the secret of a happy marriage is,' he added thoughtfully. 'I do know that marriage is full of surprises. I suppose the real secret is remembering to put that marriage first. Then children, jobs and all the rest of it — they all fall into their rightful places. Honesty, too — there has to be complete honesty at all times.' He grinned suddenly. 'Of course, you need the right ingredients to start with but you've got those.'

Helen knew exactly what he meant.

'Helen, I wish you all the joy and happiness that I've known,' Tom said simply.

Seeing that his words had moved her, and not knowing why, Tom quickly held out his arm. It wouldn't do to have the bride arriving at the church in tears — even if the bride's mother had!

'Ready, love?'

Helen took a deep breath.

'Ready, Dad!'

After all the preparation, Sarah thought it almost unfair that the day was passing so quickly. But what a day!

She would never forget hearing Kerry's excited, 'Here she comes!'

Joe, unable to resist turning round, had gazed at Helen with wonder before treating her to a rueful smile.

Their voices had been clear and full of confidence as they solemnly repeated their vows.

'I wonder where they're going for their honeymoon,' Sarah said to Tom.

'Isn't that the world's best kept secret?' Tom chuckled. 'Even Helen doesn't know. I suppose we'll have to wait until we get a postcard, love.'

She watched Helen and Joe chatting to their guests. 'They're such a popular couple, aren't they?'

Joe was holding Helen's left hand and, every now and again, his fingers traced the outline of the gleaming gold band there. 'I'm sure Joe can't believe his good fortune,' she added with a laugh.

'Quite right, too,' Tom said. 'I don't give away my first-born daughter to just anyone!'

Sarah glanced at him. 'Are you sad?'

'Certainly not,' Tom scoffed. 'As I told Helen in the car, I don't know why they call it 'giving away' the bride. I don't give my daughters away. They'll always be my daughters!' His voice softened. 'How about you, love?'

'The house will be a little quieter,' Sarah replied a little wistfully, 'but I couldn't be happier. Do you remember when Helen was born — when we opened the savings account for her wedding day?'

'What a long way off it seemed!'

'Where on earth did all the years go, Tom?'

'I suppose we exchanged them for memories.' He reached for her hand. 'Now, before you make me feel totally decrepit — let's dance!'

The music was soft and dreamlike — a chance for reflection.

Kerry was still posing for any of the guests who had bought cameras, Tom noticed with amusement. Matthew was chatting to one of Helen's girlfriends, although he kept a watchful eye on Kerry.

Helen was dancing with Joe, their happiness plain for all to see.

Melanie was dancing with Paul. They were whispering and laughing together as if they'd never known a moment's sadness.

Cassie's head was resting on Nigel's

shoulder as they moved slowly to the music, and a contented smile hovered on her lips.

'Do you think today has put ideas into Nigel's head?' Sarah asked suddenly, and Tom smiled.

'Who knows? We'll have to wait and see.'

'What do you think? About Cassie and Nigel, I mean.'

'I like him,' Tom declared. 'Although I was amazed when she brought him home to lunch, I must admit,' he added with amusement. 'The last I'd heard, he was a pompous stuffed shirt.'

'I like him, too,' Sarah agreed. 'He's very different from how I imagined him. He's very down to earth, isn't he? And how he tolerates the way Cassie bosses him around, I can't imagine!'

They laughed.

'But I can't see Cassie having marriage on her mind,' Sarah added thoughtfully. 'She's far too engrossed in her work.'

Tom didn't argue. He and Sarah had been dealt many surprises in their marriage, and Sarah would soon be getting another.

Tom knew it would be a welcome one so he didn't tell her about the conversation he'd overheard between Cassie and Nigel.

They'd crept out into the garden, that day Nigel had joined them for lunch.

He was about to make his presence known when he realised that he'd save them a great deal of embarrassment by staying where he was.

He could have told Sarah that Cassie's and Nigel's wedding plans were being kept quiet, at Cassie's insistence, so that Helen could bask in the limelight. He could also have told her that Cassie and Nigel were planning to take them both out to lunch on Sunday in order to make their announcement. And he could have told her that the wedding was planned for the twenty-fourth of June.

But he didn't.

Yes, Tom thought, their marriage had seen many surprises, some good, some bad. No doubt it would see many more, but of one thing Tom was certain. Whatever the future held in store, he and Sarah would meet it together.

A piece of confetti had found its way into Sarah's hair, and he gently removed it. She looked up at him, and the years faded away. The confetti might have been thrown on their own wedding day.

Her eyes were brimming with trust and respect, with confidence, and with a readiness to face the future. And outshining all of that was more love than a man could dream of . . .

We do hope that you have enjoyed reading this large print book.

Did you know that all of our titles are available for purchase?

We publish a wide range of high quality large print books including:
Romances, Mysteries, Classics, General Fiction, Non Fiction and Westerns.

Special interest titles available in large print are:
The Little Oxford Dictionary
Music Book
Song Book
Hymn Book
Service Book

Also available from us courtesy of Oxford University Press:
Young Readers' Dictionary
(large print edition)
Young Readers' Thesaurus
(large print edition)

For further information or a free brochure, please contact us at:
Ulverscroft Large Print Books Ltd.,
The Green, Bradgate Road, Anstey,
Leicester, LE7 7FU, England.
Tel: (00 44) 0116 236 4325
Fax: (00 44) 0116 234 0205